DISCARDED

half-human

DISCARDED

half-human

compiled &

edited by

BRUCE

COVILLE

photo illustrations by

MARC TAUSS

SCHOLASTIC PRESS
NEW YORK

Library of Congress Cataloging-in-Publication Data

Half-human / edited and compiled by Bruce Coville   p.   cm.

Contents: Becoming / Nancy Springer — Princess Dragonblood / Jude Mandell — How to make a human / Lawrence Schimel — Linnea / D.J. Malcolm — Soaring / Tim Waggoner — Water's edge / Janni Lee Simner — Elder brother / Tamora Pierce — Scarecrow / Gregory Maguire — Centaur Field / Jane Yolen — The hardest, kindest gift / Bruce Coville

Summary: A collection of stories about such creatures as mermaids and centaurs, who are part-human and part-animal, and their struggles to understand their true identity.

ISBN 0-590-95944-1

1. Animals, Mythical — Juvenile fiction.   2. Children's stories, American. [1. Animals, Mythical — Fiction.   2. Metamorphosis — Fiction.   3. Identity — Fiction.   4. Short Stories.]

I. Coville, Bruce   PZ5.H145   2001 [Fic]—dc21   00-050524

10 9 8 7 6 5 4 3 2 1   01 02 03 04 05

Printed in the U. S. A.

First edition, November 2001

The text type was set in 13-point Mrs Eaves Roman.

Book design by Kristina Albertson

for Zehava

contents

introduction: a strange mirror

For almost as long as humans have been telling stories, we have been spinning yarns about people who were like us, but not quite — people who were *half* human.

Sometimes that division was obvious, as with mermaids, centaurs, and fauns. In other tales the division was not as stark, but equally real. After all, what are elves, goblins, trolls, and all manner of monsters but beings who are like us, but not quite?

What is the source of this obsession with half-humans? Why do we still, in our modern technological age, find ourselves fascinated by mermaids and their ilk?

Perhaps it is a recognition of our own divided nature. For all our wit and courage, our striving, stargazing, and philosophizing, we are still made of flesh, still have our animal nature — and we need to remember that to live in our own skins. But we also yearn to escape our bodies' limitations. Who, watching our animal cousins, hasn't longed to be able to run like a horse, swim like a dolphin, soar like an eagle? Who wouldn't want to slip away, for a time at least, from the cares and troubles that bind us as humans and feel wild and free once more?

Of course, there is a darker side to the idea of half-humans, for in them we can also see the struggle we face every day with what scientists sometimes call the "lizard brain" — the old core deep in our brain that houses anger and greed, and prompts quick actions unchecked by thought or conscience. Once our anger, or panic, or flush of need, or whatever urge has prompted us to swift but thoughtless action has passed, we may be seized with regret. But in those moments when the animal side takes over, we act from impulse rather than thought, and the results can be embarrassing, or painful, or even tragic.

Half human indeed.

All these aspects of our animal side, both the good and the bad, were expressed in the old ideas of selkies, centaurs, harpies, and the like, and those were the kinds of creatures I had in mind when I began assembling this collection. And we do have those stories here. But writers are an ornery lot, and apt to run off in the oddest directions when you give them an idea. So I should have expected when I asked these folk for stories about half-humans that I would also end up with tales about people who are half-dragon, or half-tree, or . . .

Well, I'm not going to give away all our surprises. What I will tell you is that each of these characters, in struggling with the part of their self that is not human, faces the same questions all humans wrestle with: Who am I? What am I trying to be? What is my place in the world?

So come and take a look as our writers hold up a strange mirror, a mirror that tells us what we might be if we lived under the sea, or had the body of a horse, or the wings of a hawk.

Perhaps if you look just a bit more closely you'll find that this mirror shows not just the surface but something just beneath the surface: the wonder and the darkness, the good and the bad, the possibility and the problems, that come wrapped inside every one of our oh-so-thin human skins.

After all, we know from science that we humans are not using anywhere near the total of our capabilities. We know there is vastly more we can do and be, vastly more that we can dream of and achieve. Until we realize all those possibilities, what are any of us, really, but half-human?

becoming

NANCY SPRINGER

olor me naive, but I was thirteen before I understood why my mother always wore a turban. I thought it was just part of her artistic weirdness. I had no clue until my own hair turned into snakes.

Not coincidentally, this happened the morning after I got my first period. (Okay, color me slow developing too.) I was in a bad enough mood, what with bloating and cramps and Mom congratulating me on "becoming a woman." I barely got to sleep before the alarm went off, and right away I started worrying about what to wear to school because, see, there was this boy I liked, and everything depended on how I looked. Then I started worrying whether boys could tell when you got your period, and I felt all swollen and fat, and altogether I did not need any more stress as I lurched into the bathroom with my eyes barely open.

I was so sleepy I didn't really notice the crawly feeling in my scalp at first. But then I heard a hissing noise. And I caught a bleary glimpse of myself in the mirror.

I woke up fast, screaming, "Mom!"

She came running into the bathroom in her black silk

sleep turban and jammies, took one look at me, and exclaimed, "Oh, Dusie, how lovely!"

Lovely? Even from my mother, this was pretty weird, considering that I had a head full of snakes.

"Mom, do something!" I hopped around, flapping my arms, wanting to rip the snakes off my head but afraid to touch them.

"Now, Dusie, calm down. They're absolutely stunning." Mom smiled, all pearly teeth, although her eyes seemed shadowy. "Just look at those colors. Jade green, jet black, ruby, topaz —" Her tone changed. "Oh, dear, is that a coral snake?" Leaning closer, she peered at my head as if inspecting me for dandruff. "No, thank goodness, it's just a king snake." She got her smile back. "Dusie, I don't see a single poisonous species, and what an exquisite blend of stripes and rings! Garter snakes, grass snakes, yellow rat snakes, water snakes, black snakes, milk snakes, all kinds of sweetheart snakes, and they're very attractive, really."

I stood there stunned. I mean, up till then it hadn't been a problem that Mom was a weird artist. Famous, even, because she had a sculpture in the lobby of the Whitney, a life-sized stone man with an expression nobody could understand — yearning, quizzical, tragic, amused? Kind of the Mona Lisa of sculpture. It was called "Becoming," and it was a masterpiece; so my mother, Euryale Gorgon, was a celebrity, always going to parties and getting in *People* magazine. They loved her because she wore bizarre clothes. Mom's taste and mine didn't agree.

Especially now. Mom burbled, "They're darling snakes, really. Things could be worse."

"How?" I shrieked. Then I burst out crying.

"Dusie . . ." Mom tried to put her arms around me. I flailed away from her and bawled harder as the snakes thrashed and coiled; I could feel them through my scalp right into my skull, so creepy that I screamed again.

Mom turned stern. "Now, Dusie, don't go throwing a hissy fit."

Hissy fit was exactly what the snakes were throwing, moshing on my head and hissing like steam whistles, giving me the worst migraine of my life on top of the worst bad hair day in recorded history. I bawled, "I can't go to school like this!"

"You could borrow one of my turbans."

Oh, sure. I stamped my foot. "I hate you! I just want to die!" No boy was ever going to like me now. I had just become, absolutely, no contest, the ugliest girl in school. Make that the ugliest girl in the country. Make that the ugliest girl in the world.

Mom sighed and dropped her cheerful pose. "All right, honey. You can stay home from school today. I think it's time we had a little talk."

✦ ✦ ✦

By midafternoon, I had calmed down enough to ask, "Why didn't you tell me any of this before?"

Sitting in the apartment window and staring down at Greene Street in the February rain, Mom didn't answer right away. For the first time I noticed the lines on her face. I'd never known she was so old. Several thousand years old, actually. Her voice low, she said, "I was hoping it wouldn't happen to you too."

Silence, except for taxicabs beeping below.

Mom said, "Your father was mortal. You're half-human. I was hoping . . ." Her voice trailed away.

"Who was my father?"

She just shook her head. "He was very brave," she said.

We'd been through this before, but now I understood better why I had no father. Mom's name hadn't meant a thing to me before. I mean, who knows what a Gorgon is anymore? Mom hadn't told me until today that under the polish her nails were bronze. She hadn't told me that under the caps her teeth were fangs. She hadn't told me that she'd had wings surgically removed. She had told me, years ago, that she'd named me after her dead sister, but she hadn't told me that "Dusie" was a nickname. Short for Medusa.

"Would you like something to eat now?" Mom asked.

"No." Eat? Was she totally crazy? Couldn't she see there were snakes on my head? Quiet snakes now, but I could feel their weight, I could feel them lazily coiling, I could feel their slithery length against my neck and temples, and I knew I was never going to get used to it.

"Mom, can't we cut them off?" I begged.

Looking tired, she shook her head, "I've tried that myself, honey. They just grow back again. Instantly. Longer and thicker."

I sat straight up with a wail, and my snakes started squirming and hissing as I yelled, "Why?"

"Because they're the curse of Athena, sweetie. They're a fate. That's the way fate is."

"I hate fate!" My eyes stung, but I didn't have any tears left.

"You learn to make the best of it," Mom said. "I've gotten so I think of my serpents as pets. I gave them names." She brightened slightly. "I named one of them after Athena, actually. Then there are Hera and Demeter and —"

"Mom, stop it."

She turned to face me. "Would you like to meet them, honey?" She lifted her hands toward her turban.

"NO! You're disgusting!" Snakes flailing, I jumped up, ran for my room, and slammed the door.

A week later I tried to go back to school. I refused to borrow a turban from Mom, but I'd made myself learn to touch my snakes, and I had coated them with facial mud so they looked like dreadlocks. As long as I stayed dead calm, they would just sleep, and nobody ever looked at me anyway. I wore my biggest do-rag over my "dreads," and I felt butt ugly.

I felt so ugly I took the subway, and I hated every woman I saw with real hair. I felt like staying underground, but I got off at my stop and walked down a backstreet toward my junior high.

I never made it.

Before I got halfway there a male voice said, "Hey, cool hair."

I turned, and oh, God, it was the boy I liked, the tall one with eyes the color of tarnished silver, walking up to stand beside me. My heart started pounding and I felt crawlies on my scalp, oh no, snakes starting to rouse; I had to calm down instantly. Right now. It wasn't like I could ever be close to a guy anyway. Forget all those dreams of soft kisses and I-love-yous.

I managed to act bored and say, "Oh, hi, Troy."

"Oh, hi," he mimicked. "Aren't you the hot snot. New hairdo go to your head?" He grinned, teasing, and suddenly his hand darted toward my head to yank my hair. Only it wasn't hair. It was snakes.

Probably he was expecting me to squeal and giggle, but I jerked away. "Don't!"

"Why not?" Now he sounded pissed off. He grabbed my wrist, trying to haul me toward him, reaching for my head with his other hand.

This wasn't the way he was supposed to be, not with that stupid wolf grin on his face, not Troy. It hurt my heart, and his grip was hurting my arm, and it made me mad. I mean, my mood had been real bad over the past several days anyway. I yanked against him hard, trying to pull away. "Let me go!"

His wolf grin widened. "Hey, be nice. What's the matter with you, girl?"

He didn't even know my name, and he was mauling me? What a jerk. Trying to twist free, I panted, "There's nothing the matter with me."

"Ooooh, touchy."

"Let go of me!"

He sneered. "What if I don't want to?"

"Let go!" Without even thinking, it must have been instinct, I snatched off my do-rag. Flakes of facial mud fell all around me as my snakes reared and showed their colors. I felt them threatening, heard them hissing. Troy turned white. He dropped my arm like it burned and took a step back. But at the same time he said hoarsely, "Okay, be that way, you fat cow. You are the ugliest —"

He never got to say any more. If looks could kill . . . but mine could. I didn't realize in time, but I felt it happen as anger blazed in me, my snakes thrashed and struck at air, my eyes flared fire, and Troy . . . Troy turned to white stone.

"Did anyone see you?" Mom asked.

"How should I know? I just pushed him over, rolled him into the alley, and ran." Then, I'd been hysterical, but now I was just bummed. I mean, what's one more weird thing when you've got snakes for hair?

Mom said, "It's probably okay. In New York, most people just blink and keep walking."

I looked at her. Sitting in the apartment window again, she was wearing an emerald silk gown and a matching headdress that framed her face — her Grecian nose, jutting cheekbones, cleft chin. To anybody who liked bland blond cover girls, Mom probably looked ugly, but to me, she was beautiful. I gazed at her, but she looked at the floor.

"Your sculptures," I said after a while, and even to me my voice sounded dead. "The realistic ones. Stone."

Without looking up she said, "I can't always control it."

"Mom," I begged, "what are we going to do?"

"I don't know."

"Mom —"

"Sweetie, I don't know. I never had a daughter before." A tear rolled like molten gold from each eye. "All those years, and I never had a child."

"Please," I whispered because her pain hurt me.

"I think we need to go to the Sisterhood," she said.

At midnight we strode into Central Park. "Don't be afraid," Mom said.

"Of what? Gangs?"

She chuckled. "Testosterone-prone youths are the last thing we have to worry about."

"Unless they're carrying swords," said another voice. By the rickety light of a dying moon, I saw a tall woman step out from between the trees to walk on the footpath by my side.

"Hi, Aunt Stheno," I said.

"Sis, I don't want to hear another word about swords," said my mother in serrated tones. "Get over it."

"I'll never get over it! The three of us living peaceably at the very end of the known world, minding our own business, and that Perseus comes after us like —"

"I don't want to hear it!" Mom barked.

"Dusie has a right to know." Aunt Stheno stopped walking and grabbed my arm, turning me to face her. "Like a trophy hunter on safari, that's what, and for no reason except that we were ugly. 'Ew, Gorgons, let's go kill them,' like bagging a rhino. Kill a Gorgon, take the head home to Athena. He —"

"Sister," said Mother with fire in her voice, "that is enough."

Aunt Stheno shrank, muttered, subsided, and strode on. "Hurry up. They'll be waiting," she grumbled.

She and Mom walked so fast I had to trot to keep up as they led me up a winding path to a glade between three giant boulders. There they stopped. Looking around, at first I saw nothing except the encircling rocks, and bare trees holding the skeletal moon in their twiggy fingers.

"Greetings, Medusa," said a voice overhead. I looked up and gasped as an angel, no, a monster, a bird-woman, flew in and thumped down to stand beside me on scaly clawed feet that would have looked better on an ostrich. "Sorry," she told me, seeing that she frightened me. "I don't get much chance to fly anymore. Daytimes, I —"

"Greetings, Medusa," interrupted a honeyed growl from atop the nearest crag of stone. I jerked around to look. A woman's head stared back at me with glittering topaz eyes, her chin resting on her paws. Great golden clawed paws. Lion paws.

I felt Mom nudge me in the back. "Greetings, Sphinx," I said shakily.

A ripple of womanly laughter, approving and amused, encircled me. Atop another boulder I saw something with the head and arms and breasts of a woman but the body of a huge, thick snake. Atop the third boulder a woman stood on all fours, her hands serving as forelegs, her haunches those of a dragon. And flying down out of the sickle moon came another bird-woman, this one with harsh white hackles around her neck. And then another, spreading black wings, and more, landing on the rocks or standing among the trees until I lost track, until I heard my mother saying, "Are we all here?"

"Siren can't make it. She has a gig," somebody said.

"She's a nightclub singer," Mom said to me, and then she started making introductions as if this cold moonlit hill were a living room and I had walked in while she was having some friends over. "Everyone, I'd like you to meet my daughter. Dusie, sweetheart, you've already met Sphinx — she's a Grecian sphinx, not Egyptian, and she's a Broadway consultant. And here are the Lamia sisters." Mom turned me toward the serpent woman and the dragon woman, both of whom nodded at me. "They are performance artists. It's not coincidence that we're all here in New York; many of us are members of the artistic community."

I heard Aunt Stheno mutter, "Not all of us." Aunt Stheno worked as a bookkeeper.

Mom continued as if she hadn't heard her. "The Eumenides sisters. Nemesis is a member of the American Academy of Poetry." Turning to me again, she smiled at the winged woman who had landed first, and I winced again at the sight of those big, scaly bird feet with thick gray claws.

She must have seen me looking, because she said, "It's amazing what you can hide under a caftan." Her voice was ancient, as dry and warm as bones bleaching in the desert sun.

I blushed so hotly that my snakes squirmed. "Um, excuse me," I whispered.

"Not at all, little daughter. Take a good look, and be grateful for your own pretty feet."

"And be grateful you don't have wings," added the Lamia with a dragon tail and, yes, bat wings.

Several voices agreed that wings were the worst. "Almost impossible to hide them," said the other Lamia, the anaconda look-alike.

"And feathers," said the bird-woman with hackles around her vulturish head. "What a curse, how they itch."

"Your snakes will only itch when they shed," Aunt Stheno told me kindly. "Once a year, in the spring."

"At least none of her snakes are poisonous," said my mom.

"Good!" said Nemesis. "Little Medusa, be grateful —"

I felt grateful for nothing and I could not stand to hear another word of this. I cried, "Stop it!"

They fell silent, except for Mom, who said, "Dusie, we're just trying to help."

"I don't want help to be a freak!"

Freak! Freak! Freak! echoed away between the rocks before a honeyed growl said, "What do you want, daughter of Gorgon?"

I turned to the Sphinx with Mom's warning fingers nudging my back. No need. I couldn't speak.

The Sphinx said, "You would rather be such a freak as Aphrodite, perhaps? Or Athena?"

My mouth opened twice before I managed to whisper, "They're still around?"

"Of course. They're immortals too."

"But — but where?"

"Hollywood."

In a voice like asphalt Nemesis said, "No substantial poetry comes out of them."

I felt the great shadowed gaze of the Sphinx on me even though I could not bear to look directly at her as she said, "They are freaks too. They are freaks of beauty, that is all. And I am here to tell you, Medusa, there is more to becoming a woman than being pretty. I ask you again: What is it that you want?"

By the chill in my spine and the coiled stillness of my snakes I knew I had to answer. "I — I want . . ." Troy, alive and whole again? But no, he was not what I wanted. "I want someone . . . a boy, I mean . . . someone special."

"She wants a true love," someone whispered, and a murmur went around the Sisterhood.

"A sweetheart."

"Kind eyes and a warm heart."

"She just wants love, that's all."

"That's what we all want."

The Sphinx spoke, her lioness voice gentler. "But in this, too, we can help you, little daughter."

Oh, give me a break. I felt a strong urge to stamp my feet and hit something. My snakes reared, hissing. I swung around, peering at a circle of monster women in the dark. "Look at you!" I cried at all of them. "Look at me! Nobody's ever going to love me!" My voice broke.

Silence again. Then the Sphinx spoke. "Euryale, take her home. You ask of us what you should do yourself."

All eyes turned to my mother, including mine. Under the shadow of her turban, Mom's face looked like a carving in white marble. "Sphinx, what riddle is this?" she asked, but there was no answer. When I looked at the top of the boulder, the Sphinx was gone.

Mom did not take me home. Instead, we walked uptown along the edge of Central Park. Aunt Stheno left us at 70th Street, and then Mom started to talk.

"Before the curse, my sister Medusa was exquisitely lovely," she said, staring up Fifth Avenue, weirdly empty at this dark hour. "Her beauty rivaled Athena's. That is why Athena put the curse on her, because Poseidon's eyes turned to Medusa, and Athena was jealous. But do you know what, Dusie?" Mom turned her head, all nose and cheekbones, to look at me. "Even at the height of her beauty, when she bloomed like a rose for loveliness, Medusa never felt truly loved. She had many sweethearts, but what if they loved her only for her fair face, her golden hair, her body, and not for herself? Do you see, Dusie?"

I could not keep a sullen edge out of my voice. "Are you telling me I should be grateful to be ugly?"

"I am telling you that being beautiful may not be the blessing it seems. Athena was beautiful, but she did not feel sure of Poseidon's love. Medusa had sweethearts, but when Athena cursed her to make her ugly, they all left her."

"Well, snakes for hair," I burst out, "no wonder!"

"True. And it's no wonder, either, when a man claims to love a pretty woman. But think of the greatness of the wonder when a man loves a Gorgon."

Dawn brightened the eastern sky beyond the brownstones before I managed to say, "So it can happen?"

"It happens seldom, but when the man is worthy, it does happen. And then you know it is true love."

I walked on, silent under a sky dawning Popsicle colors, as she told me about my father. How he and she had talked and talked about art, theater, religion, philosophy, ways to change the world. How he had courted her with poetry, addressing his love to her soul. How he had waited for her to learn to trust him.

At 75th Street we turned away from Central Park. I am not quite sure when I began to realize where we were going.

"He told me his secrets," said my mother. "For one thing, he told me he was in this country illegally and likely to be deported, and if he was sent back to his home country, he would be tortured and killed. And, in time, I told him my secrets. All about me. Everything."

There it was. The Whitney. And looking at us from behind the glass of the locked entry, a life-sized stone man, "Becoming."

He stood there with his soul in his face — yearning, quizzical, tragic, quirky, and above all, loving. He gazed at me with such love that silently I started to cry, tears slipping down my cheeks.

"They came for him?" I asked. "The immigration people?"

"Yes. And his peaceful soul would not let me do this to them, not even to save him. So . . . he wanted it this way."

I gazed into his gentle stone eyes a while longer, and when I glanced at Mom again, she was taking off her turban. And oh my God, the serpents on her head — they made my snakes look like pretty little hair ribbons by comparison. Rippling, muscled like Schwarzenegger and thick as the cables on the Verrazano Bridge they reared their viper heads. I took a step back; I couldn't help it. But then I stood still and felt all the glow of dawn as those serpents on my mother's head, every ugly one of them, swayed upward to stretch and yearn toward my father's immortalized face.

Linnea

D. J. MALCOLM

Linnea climbed onto *Aegina*'s deck and thrust her sleepy face into the evening breeze. Shaking off the cobwebs of dreams, she looked up at the sky, glowing orange to the west and blending to a midnight-colored velvet in the east.

"Linnea!" Her father's deep voice called from the back of the boat. "Come sit with me. You've been belowdecks so much lately, I've forgotten what you look like."

Picking her way through the coils of rope and sacks of net, she walked around the side of the cabin to the stern. Brude was sitting on an upturned crab trap, and the dying twilight cast a harsh scowl on his face as he muttered impatient words at the net in his hands.

"Papa, what are you working on?" she asked. She sat down next to him and leaned over his knee to see the source of his curses.

"It's a net-of-thorns," he said, gently fending her off with an elbow. "Keep your distance, Princess. This brute will cut flesh to the bone." He lifted it gingerly. "It's very dangerous to the fish it seeks — and to the fisherman who doesn't show it proper respect."

Linnea examined its strange texture. The mesh was thin and spiraled, unlike the thick hemp of the other nets. "What's it made of?"

"Eel kelp." He laid the net-of-thorns down carefully and pulled a fresh length of shiny line from a sack between them. "I could haul this boat to shore with a single strand."

"What are these?" she asked, pointing at the gleaming shards knotted in the line. She gasped, and jerked her finger back. A bead of blood swelled out of her fingertip and trickled toward her palm.

"I told you not to touch it. Let me see, girl." He took her finger and examined the wound. "It's not deep, but it'll be sore for a while."

"I didn't mean to touch it. The net seemed to reach out and bite me."

"That was the bite of a cuttle rasp."

Linnea grimaced. "Won't rasps destroy the net's catch? Papa, what's this net for?"

"A doomed sea, Princess." The fisherman picked up the raw edge of the net from the pile and squinted at the next knot to be tied. "It's changed this season. I have known these waters since —" He hesitated and then sighed. "Well, for a very long time, but now they are strange to me."

Linnea looked at her father, the boat, and the sea. She shrugged. "It seems no different to me. What are you talking about?"

"Something has come. The good fish are leaving, and the few we net are sick or dead. As they disappear, the foul breeds — eels, snakes, and sharks — multiply. I believe this sea is cursed, but it's been mine so long, it's difficult to let go."

"Go? Papa, this is the first season I've felt I belong here. It calls to me. I don't want to leave."

Brude looked up from the net, a storm brewing in his eyes. "Who calls to you?"

"In my dreams the sea talks to me. It tells me I belong here." Linnea looked at her father who was staring at her, aghast. She stood to leave. "I shouldn't have told you. They're just silly dreams."

The fisherman looked at the net in his hands and shook his head. "This disturbs me, Linnea. Now, I'm sure we must move quickly — we'll sail at dawn."

"Papa, we belong here. Why would you have us run away?" When he didn't answer, she turned and headed back to the cabin.

A long shadow slid just beneath the sea's glinting skin. The sickle-shaped tail pushed the water left, then right as it propelled the huge shark forward. Its mighty head, horrible jaws sawing open and closed, swung side to side as it patrolled its domain.

Suddenly, it thrust its snout up and broke the surface. Its slate-colored sides paled as the moonlight struck its dorsal fin, a gleaming silver knife cutting the water like fabric.

The fin disappeared and two gray-blue human feet followed the surface dive. The tail split into legs, pectoral fins shaped into muscular human arms, and the ugly snout shrunk into a smooth human face. Treading water silently, he watched the boat. Nothing of his vulnerable human body resembled the shark, except the gray sheen of his skin. And his eyes. Flat and black, they watched the girl on the boat.

Linnea lay in her bunk, staring at the swirling grain in the wood that separated her from the world of water. When her father's deep, even breathing on the other side of the cabin told her he was asleep, she pushed herself silently from under her blanket and crept to the stairs.

A cool wind whipped the clouds past the moon as she walked up the foredeck. Squeezing through the narrow gap in the railing at the bow, she crawled out to her favorite spot on the boat, the triangular wedge where *Aegina*'s sloping sides curved upward, met, and reached out over the sea. Linnea loved the prow. Flying above the water's jeweled surface, she could imagine she controlled the boat, the sea, and the sky.

Now, anchored on a restless sea, the tricorn perch bobbed and ducked. Linnea absorbed the roll expertly and pulled her arms inside her nightshirt, hugging herself to keep from shivering.

Hello.

She jerked around, expecting to find her father behind her, but the door to the cabin was still closed.

Look to your future, not your past, Linnea. The voice filled her head, but this time she recognized it and knew it came from the sea. Leaning forward, she peered out over the water until a splash drew her attention down, and she saw him.

Moonlight seemed to wash the color from his smooth features. His skin was ashen, and thick dark hair fell past his shoulders into the water. He was handsome, but his ebony eyes repelled her as he stared at her without blinking.

"Do . . . I know you?" Linnea asked as she stepped back from the prow.

You have heard my voice before.

She heard him clearly, though he didn't speak. Instead, he smiled, revealing large, menacing teeth.

You came out to find me and here I am. He pointed up at her and she felt paralyzed, like a rabbit frozen by the baying of hounds. *You feel a hunger to be free. Now I offer you a feast. Step up.*

Horror-struck, Linnea felt her foot lift. Summoning all her strength, she forced it down.

Why do you fight? He hissed impatiently. *Step up!*

She pushed her feet against the deck, but they moved with a will of their own. One foot stepped forward and then the other, and impossibly, she was teetering above the sea on the prow's edge.

Dive.

Terror tore loose inside her. Her heart pounded frantically as she fought to keep her toes wrapped around the wooden trim.

Dive!

The command snapped like a lash and her body leaned out over the black water.

"Linnea!"

Brude's voice roared from deep in the cabin and Linnea's body awakened with a start that almost pitched her into the water. She windmilled her arms and caught her balance, then leapt back from the edge. Grabbing the rail, she turned to call her father when a wall of wind slammed into the boat. *Aegina* reared back on her stern and then crashed forward, plunging her prow, and Linnea, into the sea.

A fist of water smashed her face, and her lungs were crushed flat as a rushing undertow forced her deeper and deeper. She writhed, desperate to breathe, but couldn't pull her arms from her sides. Her flesh shrieked for air and something in her chest exploded.

This is death, she thought.

Struggling to pull her arms forward, the girl fought to remain conscious. Then her fingers met something hard. A large hand seized her and a vicelike grip threatened to rip her arm from its socket as it dragged her toward the surface.

Papa?

Still blind in the inky depths, Linnea longed to feel his beard and know it was he who held her, but another hand pulled her up against cold skin as she was tucked under a strong arm. Linnea stopped struggling and the fire in her chest ebbed. Her lungs no longer begged for air.

We're still underwater, she thought, vaguely disturbed. *I wonder if I'm dead.*

Moonlight from above cast a purple-green glow into the water. She turned and looked into flat black eyes.

Linnea screamed and water filled her mouth. She kicked and twisted, trying to escape from the man, the monster, who'd forced her into the sea, but he held her tight.

I am Tiburón. This sea is now your home. Do not try to leave it or you will die.

He let her go and disappeared, as if slipping behind a black curtain.

Although she had no urge to draw a breath, Linnea panicked when she felt herself being dragged down again. She clawed her way out of her wet nightshirt and tried to kick, but her legs felt bound at the knee and ankle. Using only her arms, she climbed wildly toward the moon until her face breached the sea and she floated, letting the waves massage her aching muscles. Rolling over to her belly, she scanned the dark horizon, but her father's boat was nowhere in sight. She saw the small, indigo silhouette of an island loom and then disappear as the moon slid behind a dense cloud cover. Linnea paddled toward it, sculling awkwardly as she tried in vain to kick her legs free from whatever was binding them.

Hours seemed to pass before the beach came up under her belly like a welcome whisker burn. She settled on her back with her shoulders in the wet sand, letting her body bob in the water's gentle ebb and flow. As she rested, the moon slid from behind the clouds. Linnea lifted her head, and she screamed when the light, glinting blue-green, struck her. Beginning at her hips, a thick emerald fish's tail curled up out of the water and ended with a filmy fin.

"No! It can't be!" She gaped at the alien appendage.

Flipping onto her stomach, she hauled herself out of the water until her arms, already exhausted, collapsed. Hysterical sobs wracked her body as she flailed helplessly in the sand.

I WARNED YOU NOT TO LEAVE THE SEA.

Linnea rolled over and sat up. Tiburón was in the shallows, watching her.

"Change me back!" she wailed. "I want to go home!"

This is your home. If you leave, you and everything precious to you will die.

The sun shone on Linnea's face, slicing through her eyelids like a bright knife. She shook her head sleepily and, without thinking, pushed herself back down the beach, into the water.

I wonder . . . she thought, and then remembered the same beach under moonlight. Ghastly images flooded her mind, memories of the previous night, and she dove and fled. The tail wagged furiously behind her and terror sizzled down her spine, making the fin pump even faster. Its power thrust her through the water, like a bird through the wind, and she realized it felt good.

Linnea slowed the tail and positioned her arms like wings. Lifting her chin, her whole body inclined to the surface. She tried stronger stokes, up and down, adjusting the angle of her arms at the same time. Then, with her arms back at her sides and just her shoulders controlling direction, she curved up through the shafts of light, bubbles tickling her skin.

An overwhelming sense of freedom rushed through her and with a mighty thrust, she broke the surface, exploding its foam with a great slap of the tail. She piked and dove. The green water, which had numbed her human feet, glided now over her skin like one hundred silk scarves.

A mermaid! She named it for the first time and her body flushed with excitement.

Her tail's sparkle dimmed, as though the sun had slipped behind a cloud, and Linnea looked up. A keel cleaved the water above her, drawing the barnacled sides of a large boat through the sea. Elated, she swam to the surface, just off *Aegina*'s port side.

"Papa!" she cried, waving her arms over her head. "Papa, wait!"

Without warning, her tail stiffened and went numb. Her head slipped beneath the surface and she watched helplessly as *Aegina* plowed by and disappeared.

Good morning, Linnea. Tiburón's voice purred in her head as his gray-blue body slid out in front of her.

You! Linnea forced down the panic that flared at the sight of him. *Let me go!*

Of course. He smiled. *Whatever you wish, ask.*

A tingle reanimated her tail and she pushed herself upright.

All right, I wish you would change me back and return me to my father.

Tiburón threw back his head and laughed. His mouth opened wide, distorting his face.

You are clever, Linnea, but I doubt you are clever enough to leave me. It's lonely in this cursed sea and I have chosen you to change that — perhaps, to change everything.

I don't belong here!

Oh, but you do. You have mastered the water . . . he paused with a wicked smile *. . . as though it was in your blood. I have plans and they only begin with this sea. Help me and all the oceans will be ours.*

I won't help you!

Of course you will, he murmured, swimming a lazy circle around her. *As my mate, you shall obey me. I am now your life.*

You are not my mate, and certainly not my life! Linnea snorted.

Tiburón stopped and faced her. *Do not defy me. You are the wife of the sea god, Tiburón.*

Wife! Linnea forgot all fear as her temper ignited. *If you don't change me back now, I'll pull myself onto that island and let the sun bake this tail! I'll die before I swim in this sea with you!*

Tiburón's eyes betrayed no emotion, but Linnea's skin crawled as an aura of fury enveloped her. The water between them bubbled, and she lost sight of him for a moment.

When he reappeared, terror withered her rage.

Tiburón's body had stretched by five lengths. His arms grew and flattened into pectoral fins as his legs fused behind him in a crescent-shaped tail. A cruel blade arched out of his back and gill slits split open at his neck. His nose stretched forward from his cheekbones, forming a sharp snout, and the corners of his mouth pulled down into a grim arch. Hundreds of teeth stood in rows within its frown and the flat black eyes of a monster shark stared at her with blank menace.

Pumping her tail, Linnea fled without any thought save escape. When the sea swelled behind her, she knew he was close, but she could find no more speed. Something hard bumped her, pushing her aside. The huge beast surged forward, shredding her soft flesh as she pirouetted against his raspy skin. Flames of pain licked across her torso. An immense pectoral fin lifted, avoiding her head by less than a finger's length, and she spun under the monster's belly. The shark's tail swept above her and disappeared in the bubbles of its wake.

Relief washed through her until she broke to the surface. There, she saw Tiburón's tall gray dorsal fin slicing the water on a direct path toward *Aegina* . . . and her father.

No! Tiburón, I beg you! Please! she cried out. She dove and her tail propelled her through the sea at breakneck speed. She heard a thud, followed by the sickening pop of splitting timbers. Linnea spotted the shark thrashing his head violently to wrench a section of keel from the boat's belly. *Aegina* moaned, her prow lifting out of the water as she began to sink.

Seeing no sign of her father underwater, Linnea leapt to the surface. Brude clung to the sinking mast with one arm and held a long barbed harpoon over his head with the other. The sea boiled beneath him when suddenly the mast lurched and snapped, tossing him into the remains of his boat. Linnea raced through the rubble, grabbing him as he slipped, unconscious, under the sea. A wound on his forehead clouded the water red and Linnea felt the shark approach.

"Tiburón!" she called to the beast as she struggled to keep her father's face out of the water. "Please, I know you can hear me. I'm sorry. Punish me, but I beg you — don't hurt my father!"

The deadly shadow of the shark materialized from the depths and accelerated toward them.

Please! Linnea dragged her father away as the monster's sharp snout burst through the floating debris, snapping at fragments caught in his jaws.

"Tiburón, I will stay with you if you spare my father! Do you hear me? Please, leave us now and I will stay in this sea for the rest of my life. I promise!"

The shark stood with his massive head out of the water. He turned slowly until one of his empty eyes faced Linnea. Then he slid below the surface. Linnea held her breath.

Something seized the edge of her fin, ripping it, and pulling her under. Pain shot through her entire tail and she hugged her father, bracing herself for the next bite that would cut them both in half. Instead she heard a voice:

Remember, my Queen — for the rest of your life.

Linnea's tail fanned and curled with a will beyond her own, pushing past exhaustion and misery, to bring her father safely onto the island's beach. Appreciation for her piscine half filled her heart when she pulled Brude out of the water, and then fell back into the wet sand. Her arms ached. Her head pounded. Each breath stretched the torn flesh on her belly, and at the end of her tail her fin throbbed. Pulling it from the water, she saw a bloody, semicircular bite.

"You will be sorry, Tiburón," she vowed.

Brude moaned.

Linnea pushed herself up onto her hips, lifting her father's shoulders onto her scaly lap before he opened his eyes and looked up at her.

"Princess! Is it really you?"

"Yes, Papa, it's me. Well, mostly me. You were hurt in the wreck and need to rest. Just lie still now."

"Are you all right?" he asked, struggling to sit up. Linnea squeezed her eyes closed. She heard her father gasp, and then unbearable silence. Slowly, she opened her eyes. He was not looking at her, but behind her, his head tilted and his eyes wide with shock and disbelief.

"Gods help me, Linnea," he whispered. "You're a mermaid!"

Linnea hesitated and then spoke quietly. "Yes, I was changed by the monster inside that horrible shark. He says he's god of this sea."

"God of this sea," Brude echoed bitterly. "I should have taken you away sooner. Now it will be difficult, but we'll manage."

"He has taken me for his wife, Papa. I cannot leave."

"His wife! Over my cold body!" Brude tried to stand but fell back with a sharp gasp.

"I told you to be still!" she snapped at him. "If you really want to help me you will stop shouting and take care of yourself!"

Brude closed his eyes, and Linnea softened her voice. "Papa, this isn't any fault of yours."

"It is," he said miserably. "I abandoned my sea. All these years I have waited for this to happen, hoping it wouldn't, but always afraid."

Fear crept into Linnea's heart. "What are you talking about?"

"Daughter, before you were born, I was the god of this sea."

Linnea felt as though the world turned upside down as she tried to make sense of his impossible words.

"This sea is a jewel in the Ocean Realm, and when she

was given to me, I never thought I'd want anything else."
Brude's voice was distant, as though he was recalling a tale
he'd long forgotten. "At first I had to fight to keep her,
but with each victory I grew stronger, until it was known I
couldn't be defeated. My sea, and the land about her,
thrived.

"One season a farmer moved his family to my shore.
He planted an olive grove and, after his first successful
harvest, his daughter brought a basket of black olives to
me. Her name was Lena, and when I saw her I lost my heart.

"Her eyes were gentle, but unafraid, and she made me
laugh. She teased me for being so serious. I found I
couldn't bear to be out of her sight so I asked her to be my
wife, to allow me to bring her into the sea."

He paused and looked sadly at Linnea. "I see now she
would have been a beautiful mermaid. But it was not to
be. Her father was furious when she told him. He for-
bade her to even approach the water. I raised a hurricane
and flattened his olive trees, but still he wouldn't release
her. Days went by, weeks without seeing her, and I was so
empty, I thought I'd go mad. When I learned her father
had decided to leave his farm and settle elsewhere, I knew
I had only one choice. I left the sea to lead a human life,
to be with her. Her father didn't recognize me. What he
wouldn't accept from the water, he welcomed on land, so
I married Lena with his blessing and began watching my
sea from a fishing boat."

"Did you ever think about going back?"

"I can never go back. I became a mortal when I stepped from the water."

"But you are a sea god!" Linnea insisted.

"I am a sea god, trapped in the body of a human," Brude replied. "When this body dies, I shall spend eternity a prisoner within its bones."

"Papa, that's awful!"

"If I ever questioned the wisdom of my decision, Princess, all my doubts disappeared when you arrived. You were the only reason I didn't follow my sweet Lena to the grave when the fever took her after you were born."

He reached out and took her gently in his arms. "You are more precious to me than immortality or all the seas in the Realm, Linnea, but I would rather you'd never been born than have you suffer as a prisoner in a cursed sea. You are trapped with a monster, because I made a terrible mistake."

Tears spilled down Linnea's cheeks. "Poor Papa," she whispered. "I'll think of a way to make this right." She hugged him as tightly as she could.

Linnea left her father sleeping on the beach and, without a splash, swam toward the site of *Aegina*'s wreck to collect supplies. She expected to see Tiburón every time she looked up, but he didn't appear.

Perhaps I can reason with him, she thought. *There must be a heart somewhere behind those black eyes. Papa said he was evil, but maybe* . . . Linnea spotted *Aegina* lying on the seabed, and her blood froze.

The boat lay on her side, her mast snapped like a broken bone just above the deck. Her backbone had been crushed in two places, and splintered debris littered her grave. Linnea paused at the bow. Where she had once perched, poised to fly over the waves, a gaping wound opened the boat's belly to the sea.

Aegina hadn't been sunk, she'd been devoured.

Linnea realized she was a fool to think she could find any compassion in Tiburón. *I have to kill him,* she thought. *It's the only way.* She could hear her heart pounding as she swam through the torn bow, into the fishholds.

Located beneath the fore and aft decks, and separated by a smaller pantry hold, two enormous fishholds served as storage compartments for Brude's catch. Now the forward fishhold lay exposed, empty save a few scavenging carp, which Linnea chased back out the bow. Large portions of *Aegina*'s underside were shattered, but her cabin appeared unharmed. Linnea entered through the door and glided down the stairway.

Sunlight was strained to a dim glow this far beneath the surface and, inside, the cabin was so dusky, objects appeared and disappeared like ghosts. Heavy items lay scattered along the port wall, which now rested on the bottom. One of her father's barbed harpoons had wedged its vicious tip through the metal ring of the trapdoor to the pantry. Linnea pulled it free and leaned it against *Aegina*'s ceiling, which now stood as a wall next to her.

In case we have an unexpected guest, she thought.

Without warning, white-hot pain flashed across her tail — and burned deeper with her instinctive recoil. As her frantic hands felt along her hips, toward her fin, something attacked her fingertips. Linnea froze when she realized she was in the net-of-thorns. Carefully pulling her hands free, she reached up and grasped an open porthole. The cuttle rasps dug in with each movement, but her mind screamed at her tail, ordering it to relax. She hung motionless and the net slowly clawed its way down her scales, snagging above her fin. Her tail begged to snap back and forth, to fling the net away, but Linnea held it still. Her reluctant hand reached down, hoping to touch eel kelp, not spine, but a sharp sting shot through her thumb and she pulled back. Reaching down again, she forced her trembling fingers to search for a safe place, and the heel of her hand twitched as it was pierced. She tried again and when a smooth line brushed her knuckle, she caught it between two fingers. Lifting gently, Linnea tugged the eel-kelp strand back and forth until the rasps released her and she was able to stretch her tail away. She held on to the deadly net, afraid to let it disappear again. Its weight told her this was only a corner of its length —

swimming into its center would have meant an agonizing death.

Linnea looked at the net and thought of Tiburón.

The light had almost completely disappeared when Linnea finally swam out of *Aegina*'s forward fishhold. As she headed toward the island, she tried to analyze her plan. It was difficult to imagine this game ending with her its winner, but the alternative was certain death for her and her father.

Oh, Tiburón, she thought grimly. *I have a surprise for you.*
What is it?

Linnea whirled to find his human face inches from hers. A scream rose in her throat, but she choked it back.

I heard you call. I came. What do you want?

Linnea willed her body to relax and her mind to think.
I . . . I want to know why you bit me.

The sea god reached out and took her fin in his hand.
I was angry. I'll do it again if you disobey me. What are these? He traced his finger around the wounds from the cuttle rasps.

I'm as clumsy in the water as I am on land, she answered quickly. *Perhaps if you'd been available to teach me to swim, I wouldn't be so battered.*

Linnea pulled her tail out of his hand, but his touch lingered, like a bad smell. Tiburón seemed amused by her discomfort. He took her hand.

You have been playing with something nasty, he said, examining the swollen cuts in her fingertips.

Never mind! Linnea pulled away from him, folding her arms across her chest. *Do you know my father?*

Tiburón circled her, then turned away.

Why are you going? she asked.

I am bored.

Or perhaps talking of my father scares you. Linnea swam past him, setting a casual course back to *Aegina.* When he didn't follow, she prodded him again. *You hate him because he chased you from this sea a long time ago.*

Tiburón was at her side instantly. He grabbed her arm and squeezed. *Your chatter annoys me. I should think you would know better, after our last painful discussion.*

Let me go! You're hurting me!

Tiburón pushed her away. Again he turned to leave.

Please stay, she pleaded. *I'm sorry. I've only just discovered who my father is, who I am, and I'm curious.* Her apology affected him and the hostility melted from his face. When she began to swim, he followed.

What do you want to know?

I want to know about my powers.

Tiburón laughed. *You are a baby. You have no powers.*

I have this tail, Linnea said. *And I can live underwater.*

Both were gifts from me.

I'm the daughter of the sea god, Brude. Are you sure I didn't change myself?

You are the daughter of Brude the Fool. You could not change wet sand to dry without my help.

Aegina lay just beneath them. Linnea swallowed. *Perhaps. That's why I want to see you change into the shark again.*

Tiburón scrutinized her with blank eyes.

You say you have the power to transform me — but I say I have the power and don't know how to control it. Let me watch you change so I can learn, and if I am wrong, we'll both know.

A gruesome smile twisted Tiburón's face. *I do not know whether to admire your courage or deplore your stupidity. Very well, little Queen. Learn what you can.*

The water shuddered and Linnea watched the horrifying transformation again. She wanted to swim fast and far away from the abominable creature, but forced herself to stay as he swam slowly around her. Her terror seemed to please him. The circles were hypnotic, and became tighter until he was close enough to bump her with his pectoral fin. She darted forward and punched the end of his snout. The big fish drew back, and Linnea dove toward *Aegina*.

Catch me if you can! she challenged him. *I still have half a fin!*

The sea lurched behind her as he launched in pursuit, and the mermaid cut a path straight to the cabin door. She flew through it at full speed, yanking her arms up to protect her head before slamming into the wall on the aft side of the cabin. Stunned, she had to fight to stay conscious.

The blurry world around her finally cleared and she looked back at the door. The shark's flat black eye and malevolent grin were framed in the jamb. She shrank against the wall and watched the monster swim by, her eyes riveted on the dark water where he had disappeared.

Nothing happened. She watched and waited.

The wall above her exploded and the huge gray snout crashed through the wood as though it were paper. Linnea screamed into the snapping jaws as they pushed deeper into the cabin, forcing her to retreat along the ceiling. The beast followed. Suddenly, her hand rolled across something hard and heavy. The harpoon! Linnea grabbed it with both hands and plunged it into the shark's gaping maw. A furious roar shook the boat, deafening her. The metal rod was jerked from her hands and smashed her just above the ear as the monster thrashed himself out of the boat. The cabin swirled amongst stars until she heard Tiburón's smug voice from somewhere in her tumbling brain.

What game are you playing now, my Queen?

I plan to kill you, Tiburón, she answered, dazed. *One of us won't leave this wreck alive.*

Laughter shook the water around her. *Are you prepared to die?*

Linnea tried to sort through the confusion and remember what was supposed to happen next as the boat rocked beneath her. The shark had breached the ceiling and was chewing a path toward her. Fumbling frantically, her hand found the trapdoor ring leading to the pantry hold. She jerked it open and squeezed in, pulling the door shut as the monster ripped the remnants of the cabin from *Aegina*'s deck. Linnea bolted through a torn section in the hold to get out of the boat. Swimming to the bow, she paused and looked back where the shark's enormous tail jutted from the wreckage.

You look ridiculous! she taunted, hiding under the torn bow.

Aegina shuddered as the monster pulled himself out from her belly.

Flattened against the wall of the forward fishhold, Linnea paused, expecting to see him pass in front of her . . . but the water remained still. Resisting the urge to move away from the wall and find him, her nerves stretched like fishline as she watched the silent sea.

Tiburón? Her call was quiet and echoed inside her head. Nothing. Linnea slowly swam out of the bow and looked back over *Aegina*. She scanned the smashed cabin, lying in torn fragments across the floor of the sea, but there was no sign of the destructor. Drifting back down, she looked into the forward fishhold — and heard the roar of moving water behind her.

Linnea whirled and saw the leviathan bearing down on her, his mouth set in an evil grin. There was no time to escape, and no retreat — if she fled from the boat, the monster would veer. She saw the obsidian eyes roll back white, and rows of deadly teeth reach forward as the jaws opened.

With nowhere to go but forward, Linnea charged the shark.

Her hands stretched forth to meet the monster's snout. On impact, she arched her back and thrust her fin upward, absorbing the force of the shark's momentum and cartwheeling over his dorsal fin and past his tail. The sea behind her erupted with a hideous scream. Tiburón had thundered into the hold and found the net-of-thorns.

Linnea pulled out of her spin and turned back to the wreck. Shrieks of agony filled her ears and, for a moment, she felt a pang of sympathy. The shark thrashed wildly, lifting *Aegina* off the bottom of the sea and dashing her to pieces. He swam in circles, sawing his jaws against an invisible foe, slashing his tail with fury and pain, and tightening the net with every move. The creature's long, winglike pectorals were drawn up against his body and dark jagged wounds opened beneath the piercing cuttle rasps. With his mighty fins tangled and his blood pouring into the sea, the shark's frantic fight slowed, and he began to sink.

She listened to him shudder and twitch.

Linnea! Help me! I can't breathe!

I told you one of us wouldn't leave this wreck alive.

I am a god. You cannot kill me!

But you are trapped in the body of a shark, trapped in my net. You'll never swim again.

Linnea. Please. I would have taken care of you.

You would have eaten me!

The shark's eye stared at her, lifeless, as his jaw gaped, trying to push water to his gills.

If you destroy me your father's sea will once again be undefended. What will happen when another god comes to claim it?

Linnea smiled. *The sea will not be undefended, Tiburón. It will be mine.*

And she waited for the shark to die.

The last rock fell into place and the tired mermaid settled onto the floor of the sea to rest. She had built a huge cairn over the shark's corpse. Now, this water belonged to her. And she was different.

The body that had once terrified her felt as natural as the one she'd been born with. When the shark's jaws had finally locked and life had gurgled out his gills, Linnea felt a tingle, leaving her with an odd sensation of strength. She had conquered the first invader. There would be more, but she would be waiting, and each victory would make her stronger.

Pushing off the bottom of her sea, Linnea swam

toward the island, to her father. There was very little time, and so much for him to teach her.

Papa, I promise, she vowed with the sea as her witness, *someday I will be powerful enough to tell you 'Dive!' and we will be together forever.*

water's edge

JANNI LEE SIMNER

Laura remembered the first time she heard the sea. She was in kindergarten, and the teacher was passing a conch shell around.

Laura ran her finger along the shell's pearly inside, following its smooth curve. "Hold it to your ear," the teacher said. "See if you can hear the ocean."

At first Laura heard nothing but the jostling of the other kids around her. Then wind blew, whisper soft, not in the shell but somewhere deeper, somewhere inside her. Water lapped against wet sand. A wave crashed against a rock, and as it receded, the scent of salt and seaweed filled the air. And then —

Then the shell was wrenched from her hands. "My turn!" the boy next to her cried, pressing Laura's shell to his ear with grubby fingers. "Hey!" He shook the shell as if it were a game whose batteries had died. "I don't hear nothing!"

But Laura heard. Waves pounded against stone, rising and falling and rising again. Without thought she moved to the window, aching to get nearer to the water.

All she saw outside were the asphalt and cars of a New York City street. All she heard were blaring horns. The ocean disappeared beneath the din. Laura cried, hiding her face behind her black hair so no one would see.

"What's wrong with you?" the boy demanded. He walked up to her, shell already forgotten.

"Nothing," Laura lied, because even then she could tell he didn't hear.

No one heard. In the years following, she learned that.

Not the kids at school, who kept telling her to stop acting stupid whenever they caught her staring off into space, listening. Not her teachers, who yelled at her for not answering when they called. And especially not her parents, who in the evenings turned the television up so loud it drowned out the sea sounds inside her.

Many nights when her parents were asleep Laura sat on the balcony of their small Manhattan apartment, learning to ignore the traffic, hearing waves no one else could hear, and knowing that in all the world, she was completely alone.

Her grandparents had a beach house on Long Island. That should have helped, but Laura's family only visited for holidays when the house was so full of talking, yelling, laughing relatives that Laura couldn't hear anything at all unless she went down to the beach. Even there, sooner or later some cousin she barely knew would follow, shouting into a cell phone or blaring a radio. Or else her grandfather would come laughing with her uncles, hands over his broad belly, bellowing about his youth as a sailor, when he hired on to any ship whose destination caught his fancy, before he met Laura's grandmother and settled down.

Laura's grandmother was the only one who always stayed inside, her lips pursed together, her thin gray hair pulled back in a tight bun. Mom said Grandma's hair had once been as dark and thick as Laura's, but Laura had trouble believing that.

Grandma said she stayed inside because she was scared of the water, but Laura didn't see fear in her face. She saw anger, smoldering like fire beneath Grandma's black eyes. Maybe that anger was why they didn't visit much.

The first thing Laura noticed, the day Grandpa died, was that suddenly the anger was gone.

It happened the year Laura turned twelve. He died in his sleep, which her uncles said was the wrong way for a sailor to die, but Laura couldn't imagine a right way.

The funeral wasn't so bad, but the house afterward was worse than usual. Relatives crowded around Laura, talking so loudly they hurt her ears, smoking cigarettes that stung her eyes. They were all Grandpa's relatives; Grandma had come to America from Scotland, and her family never visited.

Laura tried to ignore the noise, but it only grew louder. She glanced longingly out the house's picture window, beyond a stretch of grass and sand, to where the gray-green waves of the Atlantic tossed beneath a pale sky.

She hadn't cried, not at the funeral and not here either. What was wrong with her that she couldn't cry like everyone else?

"Laura!"

Laura looked around the living room and saw one of her aunts sitting on the couch and gesturing to her. Grandma sat beside the aunt, eyes closed, head bent toward her lap.

She looked up as Laura approached. Her sunken black eyes were ringed with red. Grandpa had once said no one really had black eyes, only very deep brown. But Laura's eyes were like Grandma's and she couldn't find any brown in them at all.

Laura shifted uncomfortably. She hated when people stared at her too long. Like when they asked her a question, and she'd been listening to the sea and missed it, but they expected an answer anyway.

"This one looks like me." Grandma's voice shook. She reached out and ran bony fingers through Laura's hair. Laura pulled away, and Grandma's hand fell to her side.

"Your mother looks like Matthew. Just seeing her red curls —" Grandma looked down, dropping both hands into her lap. "It's almost like he's young again. It's almost like he's here."

"It's all right," the aunt said. She rubbed Grandma's back.

Grandma's face tightened; her eyes sank deeper into her lined face. "How can I handle this house alone? It's too much. Matthew promised he'd clean the attic this summer. He knows I can't go up there alone. The stairs are too hard on my knees. But this summer he promised. He promised —" She started to cry, small sobs that shook her thin frame.

Laura stood there, not knowing what to say. She wished she could run away, even though she knew she was supposed to stay and help somehow.

"I — I can clean the attic for you." Cleaning was a way of helping, wasn't it?

Grandma didn't hear. Her head was in her hands now. Laura's aunt held her, saying everything was okay.

Laura's face turned hot, and her stomach clenched into a queasy knot. She had to get out of there. She turned from Grandma and ran across the room, past all the relatives whose names she couldn't remember, toward the attic stairs.

She was going to the attic to help Grandma. That had to be all right. But she felt like she was running away after all.

The attic stairs were at the end of a hall, behind a battered old door. Grandpa had never let her up there; he said the attic was unfinished. But Grandpa wasn't around to stop her now.

The door creaked as Laura opened it. Dust blew out, making her cough. She waved it away as best she could, flipped the light switch behind the door, and climbed the stairs.

She entered a room bigger than she expected, filled with overflowing boxes of clothes, broken furniture, and piles of brittle yellow newspapers, all covered with cobwebs. The bare bulb on the ceiling shone through the dust like sunbeams. The space didn't look unfinished, whatever that meant. Laura started toward the newspapers, thinking she could drag them down to the trash.

Her foot caught and she tumbled forward. Pain shot through her knee as she hit the floor. She winced and sat up, wondering what had tripped her. A nail jutted out of one of the floorboards. When Laura tried to pull it out, the entire floorboard came free.

Something lay beneath the floor, something dark and shiny. Laura knelt for a closer look. The something was covered with short, smooth hairs. Laura tried to tug it loose, but it slid from her fingers. She tightened her grip and tugged harder. The scent of seaweed filled the air. She heard the sweep of waves and the bubbling of sea foam on wet sand even as the thing came up in her hands.

It was folded like a bolt of cloth; Laura unfolded it.

The top was rounded into a head, the sides and bottom into flippers. Laura saw no seams, no signs of cutting or sewing.

It wasn't cloth at all. It was the pelt of a seal.

Even in the dim light, the short hairs glistened, like sun on water. It was beautiful, more beautiful than anything Laura had ever seen. Why was it hidden up here? Laura reached out to stroke the hairs.

The skin warmed at her touch, and an electric tingle raced up her arm. Laura jerked away, feeling a shock spark between her fingers. Somewhere far away, a single wave crashed to shore, and then the world went silent. Laura stared at the skin, afraid to touch it again, but wanting to more than anything.

Slits were cut into it, where the head and flippers began. Laura hadn't noticed that before. She reached tentatively forward and pushed her hand through one of the openings.

The skin tightened around her wrist. She gasped and pulled back. Her wrist felt numb and strange.

"Laura?" From downstairs, Mom called her. "Laura!"

Laura didn't want to go back down. She didn't want to deal with all the relatives again. She wanted to stay with the skin. Yet Mom kept calling. The attic door was open; Laura knew if she stayed here, she wouldn't be hard to find.

She folded the skin and picked it up. Her arms prickled all over, like they were falling asleep. Clutching it to her chest, she stumbled down the stairs. She glanced down the hall, didn't see anyone. Avoiding the living room, she slipped out a side door. Outside a wet wind raised goose bumps on her arms. Laura raced around the house and across its stubby lawn. She scrambled down a rocky slope to the beach and ran across the sand, stopping at the edge of the water.

Ocean stretched before her, waves rolling restlessly to shore. Water washed over Laura's shoes and socks, turning her feet clammy. She didn't care. She opened her mouth, tasting salty air. Maybe today no one would follow her.

She set the skin down and knelt in front of it. Had it really grabbed her arm? Laura took a deep breath and shoved her hand into the flipper again.

The skin clamped around her wrist, slimy and warm. Laura tried to pull loose, but this time the skin tightened and wouldn't let go. She reached down with her other hand to shove it away.

The skin grabbed that hand too. It began to move, sliding swiftly up her arms.

Panic washed over her. The skin oozed up her neck. It curled about her ears and tangled in her hair. She fought to tear free, but the skin stretched as she struggled, sticky as bubble gum.

The roll of waves turned to a roar. Seal skin flowed down her back and twined around her legs. Suddenly she couldn't see. Skin had covered her eyes. She tried to scream, but skin stretched over her mouth, so tight she couldn't breathe. It jerked her arms up behind her, pulled her legs out from beneath her. She fell helplessly forward, into the sand.

Then all at once it stopped. Laura lay on her stomach, gasping for air. The roaring subsided, leaving only normal crashing surf. Yet the sound seemed different somehow, sharper. She could see again, but the ocean looked different too, brighter and fuzzier. Wind tickled her nose.

No, not her nose. Her whiskers. The wind tickled her whiskers. She tried to touch her face, but her arm wouldn't bend right. She turned her head, straining to see her hand.

A shiny black flipper lay against the yellow sand.

Laura drew a sharp breath, tasting sea salt. She stared at the flipper, unable to believe it was part of her. Her whiskers quivered with tension. She tried to stand, but her legs slapped uselessly against the sand behind her. They had turned into flippers too. Yet how could they? People didn't just turn into seals. They just didn't.

But people couldn't hear the ocean in the middle of Manhattan either. Laura knew she wasn't like anyone else. She never had been.

She took another breath and pushed up from her waist, forcing her head as high as she could. Behind her, far away, someone called her name. The sound echoed strangely through the air, and Laura couldn't tell who it was.

Why did people keep calling her? Why couldn't they leave her alone?

Laura wriggled forward on her stomach, awkwardly at first, then faster, using her flippers to help her along the wet, gritty sand. A wave washed over her. The water went out with the tide, pulling her farther along. Laura's skin tingled. More than anything, she wanted to swim in that water. She continued forward.

The person on the shore called again. More waves washed over Laura, deeper than before. She dove into them, following the waves out to the ocean.

She came up quickly, into the chilly air. Then, taking a deep breath, she dove again. This time water surrounded her, heavy and warm. She pushed her back flippers out behind her. The water pushed back, and Laura shot forward.

She flew through the sea, slick and graceful. Beneath her, the sandy ocean bottom raced by. No one could get in her way. No one could stop her, not here.

She felt like she was home. No, somewhere better, more right, than home had ever been.

Light rippled through the water, bending brightly. A school of silver minnows scattered beneath her shadow. Laughter bubbled within Laura. She leapt above the water, and the laughter spilled out into the air. She gasped more air into her lungs.

Someone still called her. Laura dove as deep as she

could, fleeing the sound. The ocean floor dropped away. The light dimmed, unable to follow so far. The water grew heavier and cooler.

Without warning, Laura's chest tightened. Suddenly she needed to breathe; she hadn't gulped enough air to go this deep. She almost coughed, almost opened her mouth, but some instinct stopped her. She had to get out. Panic made her chest even tighter. She pushed upward, toward the surface.

Dizziness washed over her. She fought it and kept swimming, each kick more difficult than the one before. Much too slowly, the water warmed. The surface hadn't seemed so far on the way down. She was sure she wouldn't make it; sure she'd never breathe air again.

But then she burst through the water, into the bright sky. Dark spots swam in front of her eyes. She couldn't think, couldn't remember what she needed to do next. She leapt forward, toward the shore, as far as she could. Her body slammed into more water. Waves surged over her, and all the world went black.

Laura woke to sunlight shining in her eyes. Thin, salty air moved in and out of her lungs. Nothing had ever smelled so wonderful.

Wind raised prickles on her arms. She held a hand to her face; it seemed small and pale. She clenched her fingers into a fist, then stretched them out again.

Her wet dress clung to her legs. Her hair was gritty, and her shoes were gone. She bent her knees, dug her toes into the sand. She wasn't so sure she liked being human again.

"You stayed under too long," someone said, voice harsh. "You need to breathe deeper if you want to go that far."

It was the same voice that had called Laura before, only now she recognized it. She turned her head and saw Grandma sitting beside her. Water dripped from Grandma's dress and gray hair; her legs were covered with sand. "You scared me," she said, a bit of the old anger edging her words.

Laura sat up, drawing her knees to her chin. Her legs felt thin and cold. She missed the warm skin.

"I had to drag you out." Grandma's breath came in gasps. She looked tired, more tired than Laura had ever seen her. Laura couldn't believe she'd been strong enough to pull her. "There wasn't time to get anyone else." Grandma's face tightened. "If the waves hadn't brought you so close to shore, I don't know what I would have done."

"It's okay," Laura said, knowing she should thank her. But she wanted to be a seal again. She almost didn't care if she drowned this time.

She looked toward the ocean. The skin lay on the sand, near the water's edge, waves just barely washing over it. All Laura had to do was slip her hands back into the flippers. She stood. Her legs trembled beneath her, then steadied. She started forward, unused to walking, wanting to swim again.

"You should have asked me." Grandma's voice was sharp. "I would have told you how to use it."

"How would you know?" Laura demanded.

"It's my seal skin," Grandma said.

Laura shivered. "What do you mean, yours?"

Grandma sighed, a sound like wind through dry reeds. "Selkie. That's the human word for those of us who can make the change, who can live on both land and sea." Grandma stretched her fingers out in front of her, drew them together again. "Your mother looks like Matthew, but you look like me. I should have known the skin would work for you. I should have known you'd find it."

"You lost it?"

How could anyone lose such a thing?

Grandma stared into the distance, as if she were looking at something Laura couldn't see, something very far away. "Matthew took it. He saw where I'd left it on the beach, and he hid it to — to make sure I couldn't go back."

Laura shook her head, not believing the words — or not wanting to believe them. Why would anyone do something so terrible?

"Once he took my skin, I had no choice. I had to follow him." Grandma looked down, as if ashamed. "We selkies have to be careful; I wasn't careful enough. I liked the feel of wet sand beneath my feet. I never even heard your grandfather coming." She laughed, a dry, bitter sound. "The funny thing is, I didn't even hate him, not at first. Seals don't get angry, not like people, and I was more seal than human when Matthew found me. Anger came later, but — well, by then your mother and uncles were born, so I wouldn't have left, even if I could."

Grandma looked past Laura, at the water. "I wondered whether any of my children would be like me, but they all looked fully human, right down to your mother. All my grandchildren too — until you. For a while I hoped — but while you swam, you were no more graceful than your cousins. And you couldn't hear the sea."

"But I can hear it!" The words spilled out, the first time Laura had admitted them out loud. "I always have."

Grandma looked straight at her. "Why didn't you tell me? I asked you once, when you were younger. Don't you remember?"

Laura did remember a time, years ago now, when her eyes had been closed and Grandma had asked what she was listening to. *Nothing,* she'd answered automatically. "I didn't think you'd believe me."

Grandma's harsh face grew soft, almost kind. "But Laura — I hear it too."

Laura stared at Grandma, into eyes as deep and dark as her own. She thought of the others, the ones who always asked what was wrong with her, who told her to pay attention, who said to stop acting stupid.

"You know what it's like," Laura said.

"Yes. I know."

All those other voices seemed to grow small, like driftwood floating out to sea. Laura stood and walked slowly back to her grandmother's side. She reached shyly down and took Grandma's hand in her own.

Leaning on Laura heavily, Grandma stood. Together they watched the ocean. The seal skin's slick surface shone in the sun. Waves tugged more and more insistently at its edges. Laura still ached to touch the skin, to turn into a seal once more. Did Grandma feel the same way?

"You could go back now." Even as Laura spoke the words, a cold feeling settled in her chest. She didn't want Grandma to go. She didn't want to lose the skin. She didn't know which would be worse.

Grandma shook her head sadly. "Do you know how long a seal lives? Not as long as a human. I'm not sure I'd even survive the change. And if I did, well, any family I had before is long gone. You and your mother, your uncles and cousins, you're my family now." Grandma hesitated, then went on. "But you're not too old, Laura. You could take the skin. I don't want to lose you, but —" Her voice wavered, and sadness settled more deeply over her features. "But I know what it's like."

Laura wanted to take it. She wanted to dive back into the water, to fly through the bright bending light, to leap through the waves.

Grandma sighed and shut her eyes, listening. Laura closed her own eyes to listen with her. She heard the crash of waves against rocks, a higher, wilder tide than the one before her. Was she hearing the waves in Scotland, where Grandma had been a seal?

The sound began to fade. The sea quieted to a low murmur.

Laura's eyes shot open. A wave had lifted the skin off the sand, had started floating it out to sea. Her heart caught in her throat. She dropped Grandma's hand and bolted across the beach. She dove into the water, swimming hard. Her arms grasped the skin. The wave receded, leaving her hip-deep in water, holding the seal skin as tightly as she'd ever held anything. She didn't want to leave it — or the water — ever again.

She glanced back toward the beach; Grandma was walking slowly toward the house. Laura didn't want to leave her either. She suddenly wished she could be a seal and a human both.

Grandma had done that once. She'd been a seal who sometimes lived on land.

Could Laura be a human who sometimes lived in the sea?

But she didn't know how to switch from being a seal

back to being a human, not without nearly drowning. She didn't even know how to breathe right. There was so much she had to learn, if she really wanted to live in both worlds. She couldn't possibly figure it all out on her own.

Clutching the seal skin even tighter, she left the water. Her dress and hair were soaked through, and the wind blew colder than ever, but she didn't care. She ran toward Grandma, who was nearing the far edge of the beach. Farther away, by the house, someone — Mom — called both their names. Laura stopped in front of Grandma and held out the skin.

Grandma just shook her head. "I already told you. I can't take it. I'm too old —"

"I know," Laura said. "But there's something else you can do. You can teach me."

Grandma's expression turned unreadable. Suddenly uncertain, Laura added, "I mean, if you don't mind."

Without warning a smile flashed across Grandma's face, the first smile Laura had ever seen from her. With it the sadness seemed to fade, just a little. Seeing Grandma smile felt so good that Laura smiled too. Warmth spread through her, reminding her of the warmth beneath the waves.

"No, Laura, I don't mind." Grandma's smile deepened, spreading to her dark eyes. And, in a voice that was suddenly strong, she asked, "When would you like to begin?"

elder brother

TAMORA PIERCE

Shriveling. He shrank. Leaves, twigs, branches, roots, all curled in on him. His trunk went limp. His apples dropped to the earth in a green rainfall. He mourned them with tears of sap. These apples were his last crop, his children to be. His chance to spread his family with his seeds now lay on the ground, doomed to rot.

Even his tears dried until he had no more. He was dying. He had to be dying, but this was no death he knew. Without lightning or axes no tree ended so fast, in one night. At sunset he'd been vigorous, alive. The rising sun touched him as he fell, dying, from his earth.

Wasn't death a hard dark? He was soft. Sharp and slick things pricked newly tender bark. Lumps under him were his apples, his unborn children. Would he feel such things if he were dead? Even his heartwood, where his thoughts were paced like the seasons, was different. Now his thoughts tumbled like hailstones in a high wind. They were not made by normal scents and vibrations, but by things he could not even name.

Within his heartwood, among these new and

frightening thoughts, a shape formed. It was the image of a big rootless one, like those who picked his fruit. This rootless made signs in the air with his twigs. The sign-shapes blazed, then vanished.

Suddenly the tree knew big rootlesses were *humans*. This one, his thoughts whispered, was a man, a *mage*, who had just used magic on him.

"I beg you, forgive me," the mage-human said. "I've done a dreadful thing to you, and I can't undo it. I turned an enemy into an apple tree. Half a world away an apple tree — you — became a man."

When the tree said nothing the stranger went on. "I am needed here — I can't come help you. What I *have* done is place a spell so you can understand what your senses tell you. My spell also gives you the ability to speak. You won't be helpless, this first day of your new life." He cocked his head. "I'm being called. Listen — you need a name. It'll be easier to find you if I have your name. Can you think of one?"

The tree was about to say that trees had no names, but a strange thing happened. Memory whispered that a human female had once spoken to him. A visitor to his grove, she had silently touched every tree there. Only when she came to him, the last, did she speak as she took her hand from his bark: "Qiom."

"Qiom," he said now, tasting the name with a human tongue. "I am Qiom."

"Qiom," the man repeated. "Thank you. Each night, when you sleep, I'll enter your dreams and answer questions. I'll do my best to help, I swear it."

The human faded in Qiom's heartwood — his *mind*, whispered new, magical knowledge. As he faded the human said, "Some of your old self stayed with this body. You will know more about plants than most humans; you'll be strong. You can use those things to feed and protect yourself." He was only a shimmer of light among shadows. "*My* name is Numair. Again, forgive me." He was gone.

Qiom sat up and looked himself over with human eyes. He was rootless, his trunk changed beyond belief. His skin was a darker brown than Numair's had been; his shaggy crown hair was black. He looked down at human legs, wiggled stunted, ugly toes, and wept.

As the sun rose, his middle clenched. He felt empty, his head spun. New thinking said this was human hunger. If he wasn't dead, he wanted to live. Living meant food.

He struggled to stand, falling twice, and stretched out his senses. He knew the plants around him in the same way he had known them before this change, but now he also knew how to use them for food.

The apricot and almond trees that shared his grove would give food in some weeks, but not today. Their fruits would make him sick if he ate them right away. The grasses under his feet would not feed a human body at all.

Fumbling and tripping, he left the grove of his old life. He turned his nose into the wind as he had once turned his leaves to it, sorting the fragrances of plants. There, on his west side: Food he could eat right now. He shambled into the next grove, where a bounty of ripe cherries waited to be picked. As he gorged himself on them, he pitched their seeds outside the orchard. They would get a chance to take root and grow.

Once he had fed, weariness struck. He folded his new legs and sat under a cherry tree. Closing the flaps over his eyes, he fell into soft shadows.

He woke to the shrieks of humans and a feeling of pressure in his belly. Squatting, he passed dung and urine, like the wastes that dogs and other animals dumped on his roots. Human females covered from top to toe in leaves of cloth fled the cherry orchard, screaming, when he did this. As Qiom stood, swaying on his ugly stick legs, the females returned with male humans. These wore cloth leaves that fit their arms and legs closely and left their faces bare, unlike the females. The males carried wooden things — *hoes*, said his magical knowledge, and *staffs*. They hit Qiom with them, shouting.

Qiom yelped — the blows hurt. He ran away from the men. They gave chase, still battering him, still cursing him. Qiom ran faster. Once he was a safe distance away, he turned to ask them why.

The first rock struck his belly, slicing tender skin, causing sap — *blood* — to well out. Qiom clapped his hands over the cut, wailing in fright and pain. The humans threw more rocks at him. One clipped his shoulder. Another struck his head, drawing more blood. Now Qiom ran in earnest.

He kept running until he saw not another human being. He lay down in a stream until his wounds, until all of him but his chattering new knowledge, went numb in the cold water. Free of pain, he rose and trudged on down a strip of beaten earth called a road.

At sunset he entered the woods. He needed to find shelter before the night turned cold. A fallen tree, massive and hollow, offered him a place to rest. He made himself a bed of leaves and curled up inside the log, shivering as the day's heat faded. He mourned his last apples again. Would they feel as he did, green and unready for this angry new life?

He drifted in the warmth of sleep for a time. Then light bloomed in the dark, showing him the human male Numair. "What happened?" asked Numair, reaching out as if he could touch Qiom. "You're hurt. And you're cold."

"Humans happened to me," Qiom said, his voice as sharp as new sap. "I rid myself of urine and dung and they attacked me."

Numair's shoulders slumped. "Oh. You see, they expect humans to hide when they, um, release urine and dung. We also bury wastes, and we clean ourselves afterward with leaves and water. Not cleaning makes us sick."

"The females screamed at me even before I did it," Qiom told Numair. "Why? I was not hurting them."

Numair looked Qiom over. "I think it was because you are naked," he said quietly. "You need clothes."

Clothes, Qiom's new knowledge whispered. The cloth leaves that covered the human form were clothes.

"With no money, you'll have to steal some," Numair said. "It's a bad idea, but you have no choice." Carefully, he explained what he meant. For every new word he used, knowledge tumbled into Qiom's head, showering him with images and explanations. At last Numair faded from Qiom's sleep, promising to return.

In the morning Qiom found a road. Numair had said it would take him to other humans, who would have things Qiom needed to survive.

In a small village Qiom found drying-lines, each of them heavy with wet cloth fruits. Making sure he was not seen, he plucked breeches from one line, a loincloth from another, and a shirt from a third. He might have escaped the village unnoticed but for the beautiful smell that reached his nose. Warm and heady, it combined wheat, chickens, and a touch of mother cow. *Bread,* magical knowledge told him. *Food.*

Qiom tracked the scent to a plump brown circle in the window of a human dwelling. When he seized the loaf of bread, he scorched his fingers. He dropped it, sucked on his fingertips to cool them, then grabbed it again. Inside the house, a child began to scream.

Again males came, waving their weapons. Qiom ran, bread and wet clothes hugged tight to his chest. He was not quick enough: A rock struck his spine, making him gasp with pain. On he ran.

"You have to be *careful,*" Numair told him that night as Qiom slept. "Stay out of sight, watch what they do."

Qiom tried. He did, but still he lurched from disaster to disaster. He was not good at sneaking. Someone nearly always saw him — when they did, the screaming, the hitting, the pain, and the running all began afresh.

One night, tired of the cold, Qiom took shelter in a barn. In its haymow he had the best sleep of his rootless life, warmed by the body heat of the cows on the floor below. It was not yet dawn when men woke him. Qiom blinked at them as they dragged him to his feet. Somehow they had brought daylight into the barn in the hours before dawn, light captured on the ends of sticks.

The sticks were burning. These men had made a

servant of fire, the great killer! He shrank from the flames, too frightened to struggle as the men forced him out of the barn. If he disobeyed them, would they burn him too? It was hard to be calm and think, as Numair was forever telling him to do. Qiom was sure that no one had ever threatened Numair with fire.

The men dragged him to a building where a huge fire burned at its center. Qiom curled into a ball, terrified that the flames would jump to him. His captors forced him to look at a man in an orange turban and sash. This man, a priest, babbled of Oracles and gods, saying "the mad carry the god's blessing." He talked and talked. When he finished, the men took Qiom out of the village, away from that great fire. They set him free and told him never to return.

Qiom fled, sure they would send the fire leaping after him. He ran through what remained of the night. At last he fell, and slept.

Numair immediately came into Qiom's dreams, but the tree-man turned away. Where had Numair's help gotten him? When the sun rose, Qiom woke to bleeding feet, bruises, and a throbbing head. He was tired of human anything. He would finish the dying that began when he shriveled, and return to the Great Pine and the Flowering Apple, the parents of all trees. Maybe they would give him a fresh start as a seed.

He sought a place in the open, where he would be

sheltered from nothing. At last he found the perfect spot: a hill beside a road into a town. The boulders that formed the hill were capped by a lone, broad, flat stone. He could not ask for better. Qiom sat cross-legged on the rock, and waited.

People on the road stared at him. Wagons slowed as they passed. Fearing him, thinking him mad, no one spoke to him. He ignored the humans, just as he ignored Numair when the mage entered his sleep that night.

It was the world apart from people that nearly changed his mind. How could humans rush through a day without looking at the blueness of the sky or the colors of butterflies? How could they ignore the miracles of growing wheat and flying birds? Qiom had to struggle to harden his heart against the beauties visible to human eyes, beauties that tempted him to live. He succeeded. If he needed reminders of why he wished to die, all he had to do was remember fire, and rocks, and screams.

In the afternoon of his second day on the hill, a boy walking toward the town stopped to gaze at him. Even Qiom knew his dark hair was badly cut. No two clumps were the same length. He dressed as all males did — trousers, sash, shirt — and carried a cloth pack on his shoulders.

Qiom saw the boy again that evening: He was working just outside the town walls. Often the boy stopped to stare at him. In the morning, he waved to Qiom as he walked into the town.

Two more days passed. A thunderstorm broke. Qiom begged for lightning to strike him, but it did not. He was hungry, thirsty, and dizzy for lack of food and water. He tried to ignore those feelings, but it was harder than he had expected. Dust blew into his eyes, making them water. He shivered in the chilly nights. Bugs that ate humans feasted on him.

Then he saw the boy leave the town with a fat and heavy pack and a dirtless face. When the boy reached the rocky hill, he climbed it until he scrambled onto Qiom's stone.

Qiom waited for an order, or a demand for information. Instead the boy sat on his heels and opened his pack. He took out a pear. Slowly he set the fruit on the rock between them. "Good day, Elder Brother," he said. "My pack is heavy. Would you accept a pear, and lighten it?"

Other humans had given Qiom screams, threats, and blows. None had spoken gently. None had offered food. He could smell the pear. His mouth flooded with saliva; his belly, quiet for a whole day, snarled.

Elder Brother? "We are not family," he croaked. "I am no one's brother."

The boy's skin was paler than Qiom's, his nose a strong arch on a stubborn face. There was light in his eyes and kindness in his mouth. "Elder Brother is a courtesy title, to show respect. Please accept the pear and my respect."

Qiom felt things suddenly, not just hunger. The warmth in the boy's voice made his heart ache. "If I eat, it will take me longer to die," he said at last.

The boy sat back, surprised. "Die?" he repeated. "It is a beautiful day — bright with sun, cool with breezes. Surely it's a day for beginnings, not endings."

"I have begun. I don't like it," Qiom replied wearily. "I am useless. I am a tree who cannot be a tree. I know nothing of being a man."

The boy rubbed his chin. Qiom waited. He didn't expect the lad to believe him.

At last the boy said, "Trees don't want to die. They want to sink their roots deep, and open their leaves for sunlight."

A human who made sense. "I have no roots," Qiom replied, sorrowful. "And these branches don't work." He inspected his hands. "The one who changed me tries to explain human things, but he only comes at night. It is in the sun that I fail. I never know enough. People hate me. I will sit here until I die."

The boy frowned. "Aren't you hungry?" He rolled the pear closer.

Qiom swallowed a mouthful of saliva. "If I ignore it, I will die," he answered.

The boy wrapped his arms around his knees. Finally he asked, "If I teach you how to be a man, will you eat?"

A feeling struck Qiom like a stone thumping his chest. The feeling was shock. He stared at the boy. "Why? What good am I like this?"

"Everyone has some good," the boy said earnestly. "You can work. The Oracle says work is a blessing in the eyes of the god. And if there are two of us, we'll be safer from people who pick on strangers."

"Safer." The word had a good sound. "You can teach me to be a man?" If Numair, who had made him, couldn't do it, could this boy?

The boy smiled crookedly. "I'm good at teaching. My cousin is slow, but I taught him how to tie his sandals. No one else could."

Slowly Qiom wrapped his hand around the pear. It felt just right in his palm. "Why do you do this?" he asked. "Why do you help me?"

The boy looked down. "I know how it is to be without hope," he said at last. "I do this because I can." He put his palms together and bowed slightly. "I am called Fadal."

Qiom lightened Fadal's pack by eating four more pears and the flatbread the boy had tucked in his sash. "We'll get more," Fadal assured him. "There is little work to be had for money, but people will trade things for chores.

First, we need better clothes for you. And aren't you cold at night?"

Qiom nodded.

"You can have one of my blankets. If you're as strong as you look and ready to work, we can trade labor for what we'll need."

When the western sun grazed the treetops, they camped beside a deep, clear pool. Qiom went in search of mushrooms. He wanted to add something of his own to their food. He also wanted to stay away from the fire that Fadal had started. Humans were so casual with the stuff, as if they thought it would never burn them. Qiom thought he would never be comfortable with fire.

Once he'd washed his mushrooms and given them to Fadal, Qiom retreated to the base of a chestnut tree to watch. Fadal put the sausage and mushrooms on a piece of metal over the fire to work the magic humans named cooking. The food hissed and spat, releasing a smell that made Qiom's belly talk. Finally the boy put most of the meal on a piece of bark for Qiom.

He scooped up a fistful, the way he had eaten his first meal of cherries, and thrust it into his mouth. Heat seared his hand and mouth. He gasped and nearly choked, burning his throat, before he spat out the food.

"It's too hot," Fadal said. "Put cold water on your

hand." Qiom went to the pond and put first his burned hand, then his entire head, into it. The pain went away. When he pulled out of the water, Fadal washed the dropped sausage and heated it again.

Once it was ready, he crouched before Qiom, holding the piece of bark loaded with steaming food. "You blow on hot food to cool it, like this." He blew on a mushroom, then gave it to Qiom to eat.

After that, Qiom fed himself. The sausage in particular was very good. "It is the best meal I have had," he said as Fadal put more wood on the fire.

"Did your mother never cook?" Fadal asked. "What was she like?"

"I don't know," Qiom replied. "When I was a seed I was carried until I was planted. I never saw the tree from which I fell."

Fadal made a face. "Who named you Qiom, then?"

He told her about the woman, about *qiom*. "I like the sound."

"How could you know what she said?" asked Fadal craftily. "Trees don't speak or hear."

"We hear," Qiom replied. "We hear with the mouths in our leaves, and we speak in their sound. But human talking . . ." He was quiet for a while, sorting out ideas he had never put to words before. "I was old even then. Changing, becoming different. The little ghost people — *elementals* — who live in stones and streams, they said I would soon give birth to myself, to my own elemental." He felt his lips stretch and turn up, as Fadal's had. He was smiling. It felt good. "Elementals are such liars. I did not walk out of my tree body. I am a tree that walks and talks."

"So you learned enough speech from just listening to the visitors to your grove to talk now." Fadal sounded as if he did not believe Qiom.

Qiom shrugged. It was comforting in a way: At last Fadal acted like every other human he had met. Until this moment he had been so different that Qiom had started to think this friendly boy was a daylight dream born of an empty belly.

"Oh, no," he said. "Numair put magic on me, so I could speak. All these words . . . How do humans manage? I get confused. It hurts my heart."

Fadal sighed and doused the fire. He took blankets from his pack and gave one to Qiom. Then he wrapped himself in his own blanket and lay on a patch of thick grass.

Qiom thought Fadal was asleep, until a new question came from the dark. "Elder Brother, who is Numair?"

"He comes in dreams," replied Qiom. "He turned a bad man into a tree. The price of that great magic was that I turned into a man, half a world away."

"And you believe this," Fadal remarked. The boy sounded amused.

"I must," Qiom said. He closed his eyes, and slept.

✦ ✦ ✦

The next day they got work repairing stone fences around an olive grove. Resting at midmorning, they drank water and ate figs brought to them by the young son of the grove's owners. Qiom was ready to get back to work when the same boy ran by, chased by a crying little girl.

The boy halted beside the well, holding a soft, floppy thing over his head, out of the girl's reach. Magical knowledge told Qiom this was a *doll,* a girl's toy.

"I'll tell Mama!" the girl cried. She jumped frantically, trying to get the doll.

"So?" retorted the boy. "Nobody cares what girls say."

Fadal stirred. "Elder Brother, will you stop this?" he asked Qiom. "As the oldest man present, you should correct the boy."

"Why?" Qiom wanted to know. "This is not important. It is nothing to do with trees." Fadal glared at him. "Why are you angry?" Qiom asked, confused. "You said we must finish this work today."

Fadal marched over to the boy and took the doll. He gave the toy to the girl, who clutched it and ran. "Don't you know your sacred writings?" Fadal asked the boy. "The Oracle wrote, 'Women hold our future. Therefore, honor all women as you do your soul.' Honor does *not* mean torment! Go, and think on what I have said!" He pointed to the house. The boy ran inside.

Fadal returned to Qiom, his cheeks still red with anger. "He shouldn't have tormented his sister," he told Qiom. "If men aren't fair to women, women have no protection at all."

Qiom didn't know why Fadal was angry. "If you say so," he replied, lifting a big stone. "Where shall I set this?"

They finished the repairs and slept in the grove that night. In the morning they left, richer for a shirt that was patched, but warm, for Qiom, as well as for a pouch of dried fruit.

They walked into the hills, working when they could. They spent two days helping a man to slaughter sheep, an afternoon picking olives, a morning dipping candles. Fadal made sure that on each job they got something useful for Qiom: a knife, a sash, a blanket.

They had finished their noon meal after candle dipping and had gone some miles down the road when Fadal grabbed his shirtfront and sighed. "Wait here," he ordered Qiom, and strode into the woods just off the road.

Qiom waited, but Fadal took a long time. What if something was wrong? Was he sick, as Qiom had been when he ate a bad piece of meat? Then Fadal had given him herbs to stop his insides from their painful squeezing. Now Qiom found the herb pouch and went to find the boy.

Fadal was not squatting: He was shaking out a long band of cloth. His shirt was pulled up around his shoulders, revealing a body unlike Qiom's. Fadal's chest was not flat, but carried two small rounds. Now Fadal held one end of the cloth to his ribs and passed the long end around them, as if he bandaged a large scratch. A third wrapping pressed the rounded parts of his chest flat.

"Are you hurt?" Qiom asked. He saw no blood; Fadal had said nothing of being in pain.

Fadal whirled, his face dead white. He covered his chest with his hands. "Go away!" he cried. "I wanted to be alone!"

The cloth fell. He bent to grab it, still trying to hide his chest with one hand. He was breathing in gasps.

Qiom returned to the road, as confused as he had ever been in his short life. His human knowledge said that what he had seen were *breasts*, that Fadal was a female. Why did she pretend to be male? Why use cloth to hide her breasts? Why did she not wear the shell of cloth leaves like other females?

When Fadal returned, she opened her pack. "I'll make a bargain with you," she said. "We'll split the food and the things we've gotten working together, and take opposite paths. All right?"

Fadal wanted to leave? "I don't understand," Qiom replied. He did not like this. The thought of going on without Fadal was frightening.

"Enough!" Fadal exclaimed, dashing away raindrops

that fell from her eyes. "You'll denounce me at the next temple —"

"Why?" Qiom wanted to know, scared. What would become of him without her? "Temples have fire in them. I hate temples. You said you would explain things. You promised to teach me to be a man, but now you mean to leave. You make no sense, Fadal."

She stepped back and stared up into Qiom's face, her eyes searching for something. Her terror was still there, but it began to fade, to be replaced with bewilderment.

"You —" Her voice squeaked. She cleared her throat, then asked, "Why do women cover all but their eyes in veils?"

For perhaps the first time Qiom felt irritation. "I have no idea. Why do you ask me about clothes?"

Fadal sat in the road, plop, like a frog. Her eyes were huge. "You really *were* a tree."

Qiom blinked. "I said I was. What has my treeness to do with cloth leaves — with veils?" Fadal was trembling. Qiom knelt and offered her the herb pouch. "Are you sure you don't need medicine?"

Fadal took the pouch but did not open it. Instead she asked, "What do you know of our religion?"

"There is a god who is in fires," Qiom told Fadal. "I am afraid of fire, so I know nothing of its god."

Fadal's mouth quivered like an aspen leaf. "Three

hundred years ago, the Oracle came to this part of the world," she said carefully. "He spoke for the god in the Flame, our oldest god. He spoke clearly, when all others who heard the god's voice went mad, and he wrote down the god's commands. We follow what he wrote. He told us that women of an age to bear children are a temptation to men. They are disorderly and selfish. If they are not to distract men from the god, they must live apart from men, except for marriage visits. Outside women's quarters they must veil themselves until only their eyes, hands, and feet show. Old-fashioned women even wear a sheer veil over their eyes.

"My father wasn't from here. In his land, the god in the Flame is still one of many gods. Father taught me to hunt and fish and handle tools because he had no son. He died a year ago, and my mother remarried this spring. Her new husband is devout. The day he wed my mother, I was ordered to put on the body veil and move into women's quarters. He was planning my marriage." Fadal shook her head. "I couldn't bear it. I cut off my hair, bound my chest flat, and ran away. If I were caught — an unveiled woman . . ."

Her voice died away. Qiom, sitting on his heels beside her, nudged her shoulder. "What would happen?" he asked.

"Men would say I was a prostitute or a demon. They

would stone me to death." She looked at him. "But you saw. You are a man of this country; you look it and your accent is ours. But you don't care that I'm female, do you? If you didn't mind for my sake, you would for your own — the man who travels with an unveiled woman is thought to be infected with vice. He too must die because he would spread that infection. Only one explanation fits why you don't care."

"Why would I lie about being a tree?" asked Qiom. "You must admit it is a silly lie."

Fadal laughed and laughed. When water streamed from her eyes, she went alone into the trees. By the time she returned, it was too late to travel. They made camp instead. After supper, Qiom asked Fadal to tell him more of her religion. He wanted to get it all exactly right when he described it to Numair.

A man offered cloth shoes for Qiom and a cheese if they would do his farm's work for a day as he cared for his sick wife. Fadal did chores inside the house; Qiom tended the animals. As Fadal set about killing and plucking a chicken, a process Qiom didn't want to learn, he went to chop up rounds cut from a dead hornbeam tree for firewood. The chore didn't bother him — the hornbeam would feel nothing that was done to it. Qiom envied it as he picked up the ax and began to chop.

He had only learned to use an ax recently. Soon his hands blistered. Qiom put the tool down and considered the heavy circles of wood. They were very dry; a split ran a third of the way across the topmost piece. Did he really need the ax?

He picked up the circle of wood, set his fingers in the crack in its side, and tightened his muscles. It split in two. Qiom then broke each half over his knee. This was far easier than chopping, he thought as he worked his way through the pile.

He was nearly done when he heard steps in dirt. Fadal stopped nearby, silent. Was he doing something wrong? "It's easier if the wood is quite dry," he explained, facing her. "The ax hurts my hands. Am I forbidden to do it this way?"

There was an odd look in Fadal's eyes. Qiom had to search his knowledge to find the right word for it: *awe*. "You're very strong," Fadal said at last. "No, you aren't forbidden." She went back to her work. *Is it important that I am strong?* Qiom wondered as he finished the wood.

The next day they walked on. The road, nearly empty for so long, filled with human traffic. It streamed through gates in a log wall. "It's this town's market day. Towns are risky," Fadal explained as they approached the gates. "It's easier to be private in the woods or on a farm. Still, towns have plenty of work, and people will pay in coin. Fall is coming, and you need a coat."

On they trudged, part of the market-day throngs. Just outside the gates, Qiom saw a tall mound topped with strange wooden structures. Curious, he left the road to investigate. Fadal argued, saying they had to be inside before the gates closed for the night. Then, grumbling, she followed Qiom up the mound.

Qiom frowned. Why nail lengths of wood together to hang four dead humans in the air? Buzzards, feasting on the dead, hissed at him, then left.

A board with marks on it stood halfway up the mound, "These were bandits, hung yesterday," Fadal said, reading the marks. "Murderers too. I suppose they deserved hanging, but they look so sad."

Qiom shook his head over the idea of dead men, hung like fruit on dead trees. "Twice a waste," he told Fadal as they returned to the road. "A waste of living trees for the wood, and a waste of fertilizer."

Fadal looked up at him. Her eyes were sad. "Lives are more than fertilizer, Qiom," she said. "Sometimes I don't think you even want to be human."

"I don't," he replied.

They found work just inside the gates. In exchange for cleaning his stable top to bottom, an innkeeper fed them and let them sleep in his loft. Qiom woke before dawn the next day. Normally he would have roused Fadal, but not now. She had slept badly. Her nights were never as quiet as Qiom's, who only dreamed his talks with Numair.

She always finds work, thought Qiom. *Today I will find it, and wake her when I do.*

The town was stirring as he left the innyard. Wagons lined up at the gates, waiting for them to open. Qiom drew a bucket of water from the well in the square between the gates and the temple, rinsing his face and cleaning his mouth. As he finger-combed straw from his hair, he looked around. He wouldn't try the temple. Even if the priest had work, Qiom disliked the places, with those huge fires at their hearts. Fadal had said marketplaces usually had more workers than they needed. Qiom would have to look farther from the gates.

A smith offered him coins to fetch baskets of charcoal from storage; the smith's wife said they could spare another coin to have their garden weeded. Qiom was on his way to wake Fadal when he heard shouts. Two boys ran toward him, one bleeding from a cut eyebrow.

"We found a woman dressed as a man!" the injured boy told Qiom. "There was a fight, Jubrahal tore her shirt off, that's how we knew. They're taking her to the temple for correction." He scampered down a side street, yelling, "Men of the town, come to the temple!"

Qiom frowned. A woman dressed as a man — Fadal said it was rare, and forbidden. Who had been caught?

Fadal.

Qiom raced for the temple. Running, he passed the well. Fadal's open pack sat there, unattended. Here was proof that their woman was Fadal, if he'd needed it. Fadal would never have left the pack here — it carried their money, their fishing hooks, their food, and their clothes. He stopped for a moment, breathless. The sight of that abandoned pack reminded him of the human dead, hung on dead trees.

"The temple is closed to ordinary matters!" a priest cried from the temple steps as men raced inside past him. "We must cleanse our town of this demon-woman!" He entered the temple, closing the doors firmly.

Pain roared through Qiom like fire. They would throw stones at Fadal's human flesh. They would break her kindness, her patience, her stories, and her willingness to work hard.

Part of him cried: Fadal is no tree. You are no man. Escape! They will chop you down because you walk with her.

The heat in Qiom's heart burned that part of him to ashes. He ran up to the closed temple doors and laid his hands on them. They were tall, carved oak. When he tried to open them, he found they were locked.

Hurry, he must hurry, before they hurt Fadal beyond repair. Qiom set his right hand on one door, his left on the other, and pushed up from his roots. The doors creaked. He pushed again, opening his mouth to let the fire out of his heart in a vast, wordless howl.

The doors exploded off their hinges, smashing the closest benches, knocking down two fistfuls of men and boys. Qiom strode in, still howling, and seized a bench in each hand.

Men charged him. He smacked them with his benches until they fell and did not rise. Once he had made sure none of them got up, Qiom looked around the chamber. A huge fire burned at its heart, its roar mingling with the moans of those he had knocked aside. There was no one left on this side of the chamber, no sign of his friend.

Qiom moved until he could look around the central fire. On its far side, opposite the door, men held on to the shirtless Fadal. Qiom would have to go close to the fire to get her.

For a moment his courage wavered. The fire would reach out to devour him.

His mind showed him a picture as Qiom hesitated. It was a pear, on a piece of flat rock — a kind offering to a man all other humans had attacked and frightened.

Qiom stalked forward, circling the fire. Its heat pressed his skin as he walked up to Fadal's captors. He knocked three of them into the wall, then flung the bench on top of them. He dropped his other bench, grabbed the orange-sashed priest, and tossed him into the wall. One man remained, clutching Fadal as he kept a knife to her throat. Fadal's face was bruised; her shirt, breastband, and shoes were gone. Even her trousers were ripped.

"Cut Fadal and I will tear you to pieces." Qiom hardly recognized the voice that growled from his throat.

The man was already white and trembling. He threw down his knife, shoved Fadal at Qiom, and ran.

Qiom slung his friend over his shoulder. It was time to go. He raced through the opening where the temple doors had been, into the square. Ahead lay the gates to the open road. Once away from the town —

The pack. Qiom swerved to seize Fadal's pack from the lip of the well. Awkwardly he passed the bundle to Fadal. She tucked it between her chest and his back to cushion her jolting body.

Now Qiom opened his stride, his eyes on the town gates. A guard was trying to close them. More heat soared through Qiom's heart. Stooping, he grabbed a rock as he ran; straightening, he threw it hard and fast. It missed the guard's head by an inch. The man fled.

Qiom ran through the gates and down the road, past travelers and fields, into the shelter of the forest. Only when they neither saw nor heard more humans did he look for a place to stop. He followed a game trail through dense brush for over a mile, until he found open space on the bank of a stream. Gently he lowered Fadal to the ground. He undid his sash, dipped it in the cold water, and carefully placed it against the worst bruises on her face.

Fadal said nothing as he cleaned blood and dirt away,

but her eyes moved over his face. At last she stood and waded into the cold water, wincing. The center of the stream was deep enough that she could sit and be covered to her chin. She even ducked her head a number of times, her teeth chattering as she rinsed.

Qiom opened the pack. She had extra clothes. He shook them out: trousers, breechclout, caftan, and another long band of linen for her breasts. She would need that until they were free of the fire-god and his Oracle.

As she dressed, Qiom rolled up his trousers, removed his shoes, and put his feet in the stream. If she had nothing to say, he did. The night he'd learned Fadal's secret, he'd told Numair about her. The mage had made an offer then, one that Qiom had not cared about before. The morning's events had changed his mind about that.

"Numair says, if we go east to the sea and take a ship, we will come to his land. There many women are unveiled; they have respect and rights. He says, if we come, he will help us, because it is his fault I am a man."

Fadal was shivering still, despite her dry clothes. She crouched beside Qiom. "I thought you only cared for other trees," she commented, hoarse-voiced.

"So did I," Qiom said, looking at his rootless feet in the water. "But you are my friend. I care for you, Fadal." He sighed. "I suppose I am human now." He pulled his feet from the stream and rose. "It is a long walk to the sea. We should go."

Fadal stood and held out her hand. "I have only lied to you once," she said quietly. "My name is Fadala, Elder Brother." She grinned. "The next thing you know, you'll learn to start fires."

Qiom shuddered, and began to pack their things.

how to make a human

LAWRENCE SCHIMEL

Take the cat out of the sphinx
and what is left? Riddle me that.

Take the horse from the centaur
and you take away the sleek grace,
the strength of harnessed power.
What is left can still run across fields,
after a fashion, but is easily winded;
what is left will therefore erect buildings
to divide the open plains, so he no longer
must face the wide expanse where once
his equine legs raced the winds
and, sometimes, won.

Take the bull from the Minotaur
but what is left will still assemble
a herd for the sake of ruling over it.
What is left will kill for sport,
in an arena thronged with spectators
shouting "Olé!" at each deadly thrust.

Take the fish from the merman:
What is left can still swim,
if only with lots of splashing; gone
is the sleek sliding through waves,
alert to the subtle changes in the current.

What is left will build ships
so he can cross the oceans without
getting his feet wet; what is left won't care
if his boats pollute the seas he can no
longer breathe, so long as their passage
can keep him from sinking.

Take the goat from the satyr
but what is left will dance out of reach
before you have a chance
to get that Dionysian streak of mischief,
the love of music and wine, the rutting parts
that like to party all the day through.
What is left will still be stubborn and refuse
to give way; what is left will lock horns
and butt heads with anyone who challenges him.

Take the bird from the harpy
but the memory of flying, a constant yearning ache
for skies so tantalizingly distant,
will still remain, as will the established pecking orders,
the bitter squabblings over food and territory,
and the magpie eye that lusts for shiny objects.
What is left will cut down the whole forest
to feather his sprawling urban nest.

At the end of these operations,
tell me: What is left? The answer: Man,
a creature divorced from nature,
who's forgotten where he came from.

Scarecrow

GREGORY MAGUIRE

What's the first thing you know in life? Even before you know words? Sun in the sky. Heart of gold in a field of blue, and the world cracks open. You are knowing something. There you are.

As with all of us, the Scarecrow awoke knowing he had *been* for some time already, though unwoken. There was a sense of vanishing splendor in the world about him, an echo of a lost sound even before he knew what *sound* or *echo* meant. The backward crush of time and, also, time's forward rush. The knife of light between his eyes. The wound of hollowness behind his forehead. There was motion, sound, color; there was scent, depth, hope. There was already, in the first fifteen seconds, *then* and *now*.

Before him were two fields. One was filled with ripening corn. The other was shorn clean, and grew only a gallows tree in the dead center.

Beyond the fields huddled a low farmhouse, painted blue. And beyond the farmhouse rose a hill, also painted blue, or was that just the color of shadow when the cloud passed over?

A tribe of Crows sank from a point too high above for the Scarecrow to see or imagine. Their voices brayed insult at him as they fell to the field, ears of green-husked sweetcorn breaking beneath their attack. "Hey, there," cried the Scarecrow, "well then!" More instinct than anything else, and not to frighten them away, necessarily. More to announce his notice of them. But they were startled, and wheeled around, and disappeared.

Who am I? he said to himself, and then he said it aloud. The sky refused to answer, as did the corn, the wind, the light — or if they were answering, he couldn't understand the language.

The Crows returned to blot the field before him. With weapons of beak and claw and mighty wing, they beat at the corn, feasting.

"Welcome!" called the Scarecrow.

They laughed at him.

One Crow flew nearer. She seemed less interested in the corn than the others. She wore a rhinestone necklace. Her wings were infested with fleas and her eyes, he noticed, rheumy. She was an old Crow and not in the best of health.

"What's wrong with you? You're supposed to scare us," she said.

"Oh, I didn't realize."

She waggled her head. "Brainless fool."

"Brainless? What do you mean?" he said.

"Think about it. Brainless. No brain."

"How can I think about it if I haven't got a brain?" he murmured.

"You haven't got a brain, haven't got a clue, so you haven't got a chance to keep us from the corn. You're supposed to be *protecting the corn.*"

Was she being kind, in telling him his life's work, or was she taunting him for being so stupid? She flew nearer, though her cousins were ambushing the ranks of corn with fiercer strength than ever. The Scarecrow wondered if she was too old to attack the corn as fiercely as her kin. Or was she too old to be that hungry? Maybe she just preferred gossip to gluttony.

"Most creatures who can talk can figure out a little," she said. "What's your problem, brother, that you're so dim-witted?"

"My arms hurt. Maybe if they didn't hurt I would be able to think. I need to be able to think. How did I get here?" he said. "At least tell me that."

The Crow hopped onto a fence rail nearby and settled her head at an angle. She looked at him with one black eye, bright as the back of a beetle. "This is my field, I live here," she said, "I notice what goes on. But where to start?"

"The beginning," begged the Scarecrow.

"A farmer sowed a field not far away, some time ago, and from the seeds he scattered there grew a great lot of hay. Every day he watched the rain water it, and the sun nourish it, and he kept the Cows from tramping it down. It grew up bright as a field of bronzy-green swords. He was proud of that field of hay! And just before the rains at the end of summer, his heart bursting with pride, the farmer swept along the field with a huge scythe, and cut the hay to the ground."

The Scarecrow gasped. "He killed it!"

"We call it harvest," said the Crow, "but it looks mighty like killing, I agree. Anyway, the hay lay in fine thick patterns across the field. The farmer picked it up with a fork and loaded it onto a wagon. Later he bound it with twine, and stored the bales in a barn. Most of it he fed to his Cows."

"Cannibals!" snorted the Scarecrow. "He sacrificed his field for the Cows!"

"We call it farming," said the Crow. "And hay cannot talk or think like you and me. But will you pay attention? Sometimes farmers stuff some of their hay into a pair of trousers and a bright red shirt. Then a farmer might put some more into an old farm sack, and paint a face upon it. A farmer could set the sack upon the neck of the shirt, and tie it together with a moldy bit of rope good for little else."

"And then what?" said the Scarecrow.

"Well, that's you," said the Crow.

"Hay and straw and some moldy rope and some secondhand clothes? That's all I am?" said the Scarecrow. "The farmer made me? Did he teach me to talk, did he sing me to sleep, did he bless my forehead? But where did the clothes come from?"

"I don't know if the farmer made you," said the Crow, cagily, hiding something. "But he intended to, as he had set aside enough hay for your limbs, and he had chosen the sack and painted your face upon it. And those are his clothes, anyway, so in a sense he is your father."

"Didn't he need them?" asked the Scarecrow.

"No," said the Crow. "Not after a while. Before he could finish you, he fell sick. I suppose he must have died. No man needs his clothes after he's died."

"What does *after* mean?" said the Scarecrow, who was too new to understand befores and afters.

"It means the *next* that follows the *now,* or the *now* that follows the *once.*"

"I wish I had a brain," said the Scarecrow. "I understand a man falling sick and dying, but I do not understand befores and afters."

"The last time I laid eyes on him, I was perched on his windowsill, being nosy. I saw him tossing and turning with a fever. It seemed bad. I know he must have died, for if he had not, he would be running to berate you for letting us Crows eat all the corn. But he is dead, and you are all alone. That's too bad, but it can't be helped. I suppose his farmer neighbors took the clothes off his dead body and finished dressing you, and set you on your stake to do the job you were made to do. Too bad you can't do it very well. And now I will stop chatting and go eat some corn myself." Off she flew, in a fluttery, palsied manner, her jewelry flashing in the sun like splashes of fountain. The Scarecrow could see that she had been waiting to peck at ears of corn already cut open by the stronger crows.

"Stop," called the Scarecrow, "stop!" He did not mean for her to stop eating the corn, for he did not care. He meant to stop her from leaving. But she didn't listen.

The Crows made a mess of the cornfield. The Scarecrow knew that the old Crow must have been telling the truth, for no farmer came running from the nearby house to scold him for the damage. But even more damage lay in store. The next day the sky turned hugely purple. Mountainous clouds swept over, dragging along the ground a smoky funnel of wind. The remaining stalks were flattened. When the Crows returned, they had to settle their spiky pronged feet in the complicated floor of leaves and stalks, and hunt with lowered heads for what corn could still be found.

"Stop," cried the Scarecrow, "look out! Beware!" But he was not trying to protect the corn. He had seen a different danger approaching his friend the Crow. Her hearing was not what it once must have been so she wasn't aware. Her head was down, hunched in her collar of fine glints, digging for an especially rich ear of corn. From a hump of green rubble launched a missile of red fur and black leather boots, and teeth as sharp as the points of rhinestones. Sharper even. The other Crows escaped in an explosion of noisy wings and terrified cries, but the old Crow was too slow. She fell beneath clever paws and hungry jaws, and the jewelry made a bright exclamation mark in the air before it dropped to the ground.

"Yum," said the Fox, after he had finished his meal. "Yes, she was good. But I feel like a little something more." He tried his teeth on the necklace, but it did not appeal to his taste. So the Fox stood up in his black leather boots, and though he could see farther than he would have had the corn not fallen in the wind, he still could not find a suitable sweet morsel to finish his meal. "Strawhead," said the Fox, "you are higher than I. Can you see anything sweet for me to go after?" He licked his chops.

"What do you mean, *after*?" said the Scarecrow, a bit wary, but still curious.

"After?" said the Fox. "*After*? After means *toward*. I go

after the Crow, and I get her. I go after my Vixen, and I get her. I go after what I want. What do you want?"

"To understand," said the Scarecrow, sighing.

"Ah, knowledge is sweet, too," said the Fox. He resigned himself to conversation rather than dessert, and he circled himself into a coil of Fox, where he could see how his hind legs ended so magnificently in black leather boots. He settled his bush over himself like a blanket. Then he put his chin upon his front paws and looked up at the Scarecrow. His eyes began to close.

"It seems a brutal world," said the Scarecrow.

"Doesn't it though," said the Fox appreciatively.

"You speak as if you know me," said the Scarecrow.

"I believe I know your clothes," said the Fox. "I recognize them. Your clothes make you seem quite familiar. I am happy not to be running from the farmer who used to wear them. When he would see me in his henhouse he would run for a weapon. But now the clothes have survived the man, for he must be dead. Otherwise he would be out here harvesting what is left of his flattened crop of corn. I notice that his clothes are capable of nothing more than housing straw — rather chatty straw, to my surprise, but straw nonetheless."

"He died of a terrible illness, I hear," said the Scarecrow.

"Is that so? Not what I heard." The Fox purred softly at the thought of treachery. "In all likelihood he died over there on the gallows tree. He was to be hung by the neck until he was dead," said the Fox. "The farmer's friendly neighbors intended to break his neck just as I broke the neck of Madame Crow a few minutes ago."

"But why?" said the Scarecrow, alarmed.

"Before you were born, the farmer had gone off to another village to buy some seedcorn," said the Fox. "When he came back he fell deeply ill. Folks round here are afraid of the plague, and none of them would tend him. He tossed and turned in a raging fever. But somehow he survived, and believed himself to be recovered. He went to the well in the center of the village and greeted all his neighbors — though somewhat coldly, I'll wager, since they had not come to his help. Then a terrible misfortune occurred. Within days the villagers he met succumbed to fevers and fits, and some of them died. The ones who survived blamed him for the outbreak of sickness. They went after him."

"After him," said the Scarecrow, trying hard to understand.

"They said he had caused the death of their loved ones," said the Fox. "They said he had infected them on purpose, so that other families would not have the help to bring in their corn, and he alone would prosper with a good crop. They came after him with pitchforks and accusations. The farmer was not yet well enough to run

away with any speed. They caught him in the middle of
the corn. I saw them trap him; I was hiding in the weevily
shadows, watching. They went to hang him, much as you
are hung there on your stake. I would have stayed to watch
the execution, but a sudden summer storm came up, and
I fled to my hole. But I suppose they did their job and
gave him his death."

"Did he not ask for their charity?" said the Scarecrow.

"Oh, anyone can ask," said the Fox. "No doubt the
Crow would have asked for my charity if she'd been able
to squeeze breath through her gullet. But charity doesn't
satisfy the stomach, does it?"

The Scarecrow didn't know. He tried to close his eyes
to squeeze out the sight of the gallows tree in the next
field over, but his eyes were painted open. He tried not
to listen to the Fox, but his ears were painted open. He
tried to still the beating in his chest, but he couldn't; this
was because a family of Mice had discovered the Scarecrow and were exploring him as a possible home. It was
both uncomfortable and slightly embarrassing to have
Mice capering about inside his clothes.

"I suggest you should look for lodging elsewhere," said
the Scarecrow in as low a voice as he could manage,
"for there is a Fox nearby who likes to go after small creatures."

The Mice took heed and removed themselves to a safer
neighborhood. The Fox, nearly asleep, began to laugh

softly. "Charity is so appealing in the young," he said. Soon thereafter he began to snore.

The Scarecrow had no choice but to look at the farm-house, the fields, the gallows tree, the hill beyond them all. The world seemed a bitter place, arranged just so: fields, gallows, house, and hill.

Then around the edge of the hill came a girl and a dog. They were both walking briskly, with a little skip in their step, and from time to time the dog would run ahead and sniff at the seams of the world here and there. The Fox was deep in his dream and the dog would soon be upon him. "Stop!" cried the Scarecrow.

The Fox bolted upright from his sleep and his neck twisted around so his ruff stood out like a brush. He saw the child and the dog. Instinctively ready to flee, the Fox took just enough time to glance up at the Scarecrow as if to say: *Why? Why do you save me, when you disapprove of how I am, when you disapprove of how the world is? Why do you bother?*

But he could not take the time to voice the questions, for the dog was almost upon him, and the Fox disappeared in a streak of smoke-red against the green-and-gold wreckage of the cornfield. He vanished so quickly that he left behind his pair of handsome black leather boots.

The dog barked. It seemed unable to make a sensible remark, and the Scarecrow by now was not inclined to question it anyway. The Scarecrow did not know why he had alerted the Fox to danger. Were the clothes that the Scarecrow was born into the clothes of a kindly man or a terrible one? Did it matter who the farmer had been, did that shape who the Scarecrow might be? What manner of creature, what quality of spirit, what variety of soul?

It was very troubling. The Scarecrow merely watched as the girl approached. By now he was not sure that he cared to know any more about the world.

The girl wore her hair in pigtails. She was clothed in a sensible dress with an apron tied neatly behind in a bow. She wore neither rhinestone necklace nor black leather boots, but her shoes were glittering in the afternoon sun. "What's that, then?" she said to the dog in a fond voice. "Did you smell something of interest?"

The dog circled about beneath the Scarecrow's pillar, and looked up and barked.

"Why, a Scarecrow," said the girl. "What do you know?"

Since the Scarecrow knew very little indeed, he did not answer.

"I should like to know which is the best way to proceed," said the girl, almost to herself. "The road divides here, and we could go this way, or that way."

The Scarecrow knew only the house, the fields, the gallows tree, the hill.

"Perhaps it doesn't matter, though," continued the girl, musing. "We didn't choose to come here, after all, so perhaps any choice we make from here has the chance of being the right one."

"What does that mean?" said the Scarecrow.

The girl gave a little start and the dog went and cowered behind the basket she had set down. "I'm a foreigner," she said, "an accidental visitor, and I do not know my way."

"I mean, *after all,*" said the Scarecrow. "I do not understand befores and afters. What does *after all* mean? It sounds important."

"After all?" said the girl. She put her head to one side. "It means, when everything is thought about, what you can then conclude."

"If you can't think," said the Scarecrow, "can you have an after all?"

"Of course," said the girl, "but thinking helps."

"I should like to learn to think," said the Scarecrow. "I should like to know about this more, before the world seems too dark to bear."

"Would you like to get down?" said the girl.

This had never occurred to the Scarecrow yet. "May I?" he said.

"I will loosen you off your hook if I can reach," said the girl, but she couldn't. Still, she didn't give up. She wandered across the field to the farmhouse. The Scarecrow watched her knock on the door, and when there was no answer, he saw her enter. Before long she returned with a little chair. She stood on it and worked at the nail on which the Scarecrow hung. She managed to bend it down, and off he slid, into a heap on the ground.

It felt good to move!

"Whyever did you help me?" he asked.

"Whyever not?" she said, and he didn't know the answer since he didn't know much. But he grinned, for it was fun to be asked, and maybe if she asked him again someday, he would have an answer ready.

"How do you come to be a talking Scarecrow?" she said.

"I don't know," he said. "How do you come to be a talking girl?"

"I'm sure I have no idea," said the girl. "I was born this way."

"So was I," said the Scarecrow. "But my clothes were given me by a dead man, I hear."

He told the girl the story of the farmer who had been treacherously ill, and then had shared his disease with his neighbors, though by chance or intention it could not be said for sure. The Scarecrow told how the neighbors had fallen upon the farmer and killed him for the crime.

The girl looked doubtful. "Who tells you such a grim tale?" she said.

"A Crow, rest her soul, and a Fox, luck preserve him," said the Scarecrow.

The girl looked sadly at the Scarecrow. "You believe everything you're told?" she said.

"I haven't been told a whole lot yet," the Scarecrow admitted. "I'm only two days old, I think."

The girl said, "Wait here while I return the chair to where I found it." And off she went with a thoughtful expression on her face. Her dog followed her with a cheery wag of his tail.

The Scarecrow trusted that she would return. And return she did. She had a calmer look on her face. "The Crow did not know and the Fox did not know," she said warmly. "But I can read, and I do know. I saw a letter on the table in the farmhouse. It was a letter written by the farmer."

"Yes?" said the Scarecrow.

"The letter said, 'To my neighbors: You will think that I have died. But I have not. This spring when I went over the hill to buy my seedcorn, I fell in love with a woman there. On my return, I had hoped to sow my fields quickly and then go back to marry her, and bring her here to live, but my sickness prevented my traveling. When you caught me and brought me so close to death on the gallows tree, I thought that was the end. But fate would have it otherwise. The storm came up and you all ran for safety. Then appeared my beloved, who had worried because I hadn't returned to her. She had come to find out why, and she had seen you gather, and hid herself in the corn. Seizing her chance, she leapt up and cut me down. So today I am going to marry her. I will not come back to this farm, for I need to make myself a happily ever after somewhere far from here. I have dressed myself in brand-new clothes to make her pleased with her choice. Here are my old clothes. Please use them for the public good and make a Scarecrow to protect the corn from the Crows. It is your corn now, as it always would have been whenever you needed it. Good—bye.'"

The Scarecrow felt his spirits lift up. "So the owner of these clothes was a man who cared for the well-being of his neighbors, even those who had tried to kill him?"

"I do believe," said the girl, "an unusual man with a good heart."

"We should go tear down the gallows tree in the middle of the next field," said the Scarecrow, "so the neighbors may not try such a scheme again."

The girl peered at it with her hand over her eye. "That is not usually a gallows tree," she decided. "It is really just a pole for you to rest upon when that field is ready to be planted with another crop of corn."

The Scarecrow said, "So the stories of the Crow and the Fox were wrong."

"The Crow and Fox were not wrong," said the girl, "they just did not know what came after." She smiled at the Scarecrow and began to play with bits of corn husk. She made a dolly from an ear of corn, and twisted the leaves of cornstalks to make arms and legs. She dressed it in a rhinestone necklace and a pair of black leather boots.

The Scarecrow waited for the dolly to speak. It was no less than he was, some dead agricultural matter dressed up in human clothes. But it did not speak or move as he did.

"Why does it not tell us something?" he asked the girl. "Why am I alive and it is not?"

"I do not know," said the girl. "I am young too. I do not know why I have arrived here in this strange land, where Scarecrows can talk. There is a lot I don't know. It was all winds and noises when I came —"

This reminded the Scarecrow of the day of his awakening — the day before yesterday. He nodded, for the first time knowing something to be true because of his own experience of it. "And lights," he said.

"Yes, and lights," said the girl. "Lights and darks. And suddenly I was here, where everything seems strange. And I don't know why. Like the Fox and the Crow, I don't know the whole story yet. But that's a good reason to go on, don't you think?"

"Go where?" said the Scarecrow.

"Go forward," said the girl. "See something. Learn something. Figure it out. We won't ever get the whole thing, I bet, but we'll get something. And then we'll have something to tell when we're old about what happened to us when we were young."

"Now?" said the Scarecrow. "Can you tell it now?"

"After," said the girl. "We have to have the *before* first, and that's life."

"And what's life?" said the Scarecrow.

"Moving," said the girl. "Moving on. Shall we move on? Will you come with me?"

"Yes," said the Scarecrow. "For the sake of knowing some more about this, of developing my brains so I can bear this mystery better." Straw limbs and human clothes, perhaps, but still hungry for a life to live before so that there could be a story to tell after.

"Which way shall we go?" said the girl.

"Not toward the fields, the house, the hill, the gallows tree," said the Scarecrow. "Let's go in the direction we have not yet gone."

"Good enough for me," said the girl. She left the corn dolly for some other child to find. Then she picked up her basket and the dog came running to her heels. Now that the Scarecrow was down on the ground, he could see that the two fields that made up his world so far were divided by a road paved with yellow brick.

"This way," said the girl. And she and the Scarecrow turned their heads toward the west.

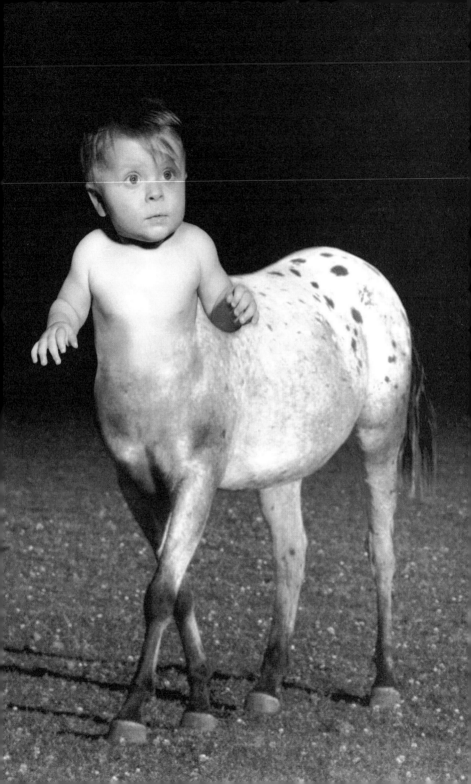

centaur field

JANE YOLEN

Our old pony Agora went into labor on Saturday afternoon when I was at the stables cleaning out stalls for my mom. I heard Agora's rough breathing and ran for the phone. Mom had said to call the vet the minute anything began.

It had been an odd pregnancy from the start. Agora had never been bred before. In fact, she hadn't been bred this time either. At least not on purpose. Martha McKean, our farmhand, thought one of the stallions from the Suss farm down the road had gotten loose and found Agora out in the field one night.

Me — I figured it had as much to do with that wild night of meteor showers in September as some prized Suss Morgan stallion jumping fences and falling for an old Shetland pony. I was up half the night watching the star display with my father's old telescope and had never seen anything like that before. Waterfalls of stars shooting across the sky.

Besides, Mr. Suss would have complained loud and long if any of his stallions had gotten out, and he never said a word.

I ran back to watch Agora, knowing the vet was now on the way. He'd said that this being her first pregnancy, and Agora being old for a pony, things should move very slowly and not to worry and he'd be right over. But while his words said calm things, his voice was tight and abnormally high. So he was worried.

Me too.

Agora was lying down and Martha was sitting in the straw by her side. She had Agora's head in her lap and the two of them looked like a couple of old friends conversing. Martha's not very good with people, Mom says, but she's great with ponies. All the while, Agora's belly was bouncing about in a really odd way.

"I called Dr. Herks," I said. "He's on his way."

"Good," Martha said, never looking up. She hardly ever made eye contact with anyone so I wasn't hurt or anything.

"He sounded . . . a bit nervous," I added.

"He should be," Martha said, still looking down at the pony. But her voice was quiet, soothing, meant for Agora, not me.

"Anything more I can do?" I asked.

"Boil water," she said.

"Really?"

"An old joke." She chuckled. "Doctors used to have expectant dads do it, just to keep them busy and out of the way. I bet your dad did that."

"I wouldn't know," I said, not wanting to visit that particular hurt. But I got the hint and went back to cleaning out stalls.

The horses knew something was up, though; Muffin, who never did anything of the sort, slammed down on my foot not once but twice. Lucky I was wearing boots and not my usual sneakers. And Wester, normally the sweetest of geldings, tried to rip a hank of hair out of my head. I left the barn gladly when I heard the vet's car drive up.

I liked Dr. Herks a lot. Though he has a young face that is handsome in certain lights, there are wrinkle lines on his forehead that look like the stripes in a flag. And I had a feeling that he was sweet on my mom.

"How's it going?" he asked.

"I'm supposed to be boiling water," I said. He's always willing to talk to me, unlike some grown-ups around the farm who think kids are to be ordered, not asked.

He smiled a little. "I'll need all the help I can get."

I nodded. "I'll give you all I got," I said. Then I matched him step for step to the stall, which wasn't easy, because he's a long-legged man.

We got to the stall and I looked in on Agora. "Jeeze . . ." I whispered.

Dr. Herks just breathed loudly, walked in and knelt down by Martha's side.

She was holding the new colt.

Or whatever it was.

"Jeeze . . ." I said again. Because it was only a colt from the tail to the trunk. Where the horse's shoulders and neck and head should have been, it looked just like a little boy, with dark curly hair and a big grin. His teeth were even-spaced baby teeth. "Jeeze."

"Centaur," said Martha to me, to the vet. "I never . . ."

"No one never," said the vet, which was totally un-grammatical but perfectly understandable. And then he fainted. Which was not understandable at all, seeing as he was not just a vet, but a Vet, that is he had fought in the Gulf War and been decorated for bravery but is now a member of the same Quaker Meeting we are and is totally against war of any kind.

"Get your mother," said Martha. It was not clear if she meant for help with the centaur or with Dr. Herks. Whichever, I ran out of there. I think I may have screamed all the way to the house. Or else it was a very loud whimper. Mom came out in a rush and when she saw what had been born in the stall, she said "Jeeze . . ." just like I had. She put her fist partway in her mouth. I hadn't seen her like that since . . . well not in a long while.

The whole time, the only really calm one was Agora, who took to licking her little centaur colt. She made no distinction between the horse part and the boy part. He was simply hers all over. When she got to his face, he giggled and pushed her away, then giggled again. She got slowly to her feet and he struggled to get up as well. Then, like any newborn colt, he began to nurse, his hands alternately stroking and kneading her sides.

Dr. Herks, starting to come to, saw the centaur, and looked ready to pass out again. Mom put her hands under his arms and I took his feet and we dragged him out into the driveway.

"If you're going to faint again, Gerry, do it where you won't disturb them," Mom said smartly. And I remembered that she'd said something of that sort to Dad right before he left.

Gerry didn't leave, he got to his feet, as wobbly as the colt, and thoroughly embarrassed about fainting.

"What do we do now?" he asked.

Mom took a deep breath, almost as if to mentally sort herself out. Then she said, "Well, what we don't do is ignore it or turn our backs on it. What we don't do is call World Wide News or *The Star* or CNN or Oprah or anyone like that." She tried a smile. It didn't work. "At least not until that colt is old enough to stand the crowds. Agreed?" She held out her hand.

"Agreed," he said and took her hand.

For a moment that's where things remained. But we were all thinking about later, when the other owners came to see their horses. And the kids came for riding lessons. And Karen who helps clean stalls arrived. And George who takes care of all the tack and delivers the feed drove up in his old pickup. And the mailman. And the UPS man. And the papergirl. And . . .

That's when Martha found us. "I think we should put them in the quarantine stall," she said, looking somewhere between Mom and Dr. Herks. "Hang blankets on the bars so no one can see in. Give out the word that the vet has said . . ."

Dr. Herks drew himself up, shaking himself at the same time like an old dog after a bath. "Tell them the vet has warned that it would be dangerous for both Agora and her new colt to be bothered. Tell them that I am afraid of *Puericentaurcephalitis* spreading to any person or horse coming in contact with them. But emphasize that there is no danger as long as they are left strictly alone."

"What's that?" Mom asked. "*Puericentaurcephalitis*. I've never heard of it."

Dr. Herks smiled an almost smile. "I just made it up," he said. "It's Latin for boy-centaur-disease. I'll write it down if Arianne will go and get my bag from the stall."

I went back into the barn, snatched up the black bag, and saw that the little colt boy was now lying down in the bedding, napping, with a thumb like a cork stuck firmly in his mouth.

For about a week the cover story held. No one dared go near the quarantine stall. But no one wanted me or Mom or Dr. Herks near their horses either. Just in case. It was clear that sooner or later — and probably sooner — all of our boarders were going to take their horses to another stable. And the kids would go elsewhere for lessons. We sure couldn't afford that to happen, though there were some I'd pay to see leave. But it was already a guess at the end of each month as to whether Mom could manage all the bills.

Martha and I shared most of the cleanup work in Agora's stall, but Mom took to sleeping there at nights. I found her one morning when I went out to do my chores. She was still asleep and the little boy's head was cradled in the crook of her arm. If I squinted my eyes and didn't look at the rest of him, he looked almost normal. Almost human.

But things had gotten seriously weird at the barn, not to mention seriously difficult, what with little money coming in. So we called a sitting-at-the-kitchen-table meeting: Martha, Dr. Herks, Mom, and me.

For a minute we all looked at one another, too glazed over from work and secrets to speak. The money was only a part of the issue. There were more serious matters at stake.

Then I just blurted it out. The thing that had bothered me from the beginning. "How come the human part of the centaur isn't a baby?"

They all glared at me.

"I mean," I said slowly, as if speaking in a different language, "why is he a little boy? And not only that but . . ."

Before I could add that he was growing much faster than any kid I had ever seen, they all started talking at once.

Mom said, "Maybe it's because . . . oh, what do I know?"

Martha said, "I haven't the foggiest . . ."

And Dr. Herks said the only sensible thing. "Because horses mature faster than humans, and for the boy-half to stay in sync with the horse-half, it has to grow lots faster than normal."

I wanted to ask something more, this time about digestion, I think. Martha was trying to shush me so we could talk about the real possibility of losing the farm. And Mom, well she just looked tired and sad, the way she had right before Dad left.

Just then Mrs. Angotti and her little boy Joey marched into the house without even knocking. Her daughter Angela was probably off on a trail ride kicking black-and-blue marks in Monument's massive sides. Neither Mom nor I really liked Angela or Joey, but their whole family took lessons, and there were lots of cousins we could count on, which helped keep the farm in the black. Barely.

Mrs. Angotti had hold of Joey's arm, like she was angry with him. But when she spoke all her anger went outward, in a kind of loud, unfocused way. She always talks in run-on sentences, the kind my English teacher never lets us use in essays. But when Mrs. Angotti spoke, it was also a kind of miracle because I don't think she ever breathes between paragraphs.

She said: "So Joey went over to that stall, like I said he wasn't to do, but he had to anyway — he's like his father, can't ever listen to what he's been told — and he comes back with a face white as my mother-in-law's pasta, saying something about a freak. Now I would have slapped him except the one thing Joey doesn't do bad is to tell lies, so I went over, even though it was quarantined — which is a strange word if you ask me, but so are most *q* words like quince and Quernavaca and cuneiform — or is that with a *c*? — and I looked where he was pointing."

"You didn't!" Mom said, which was unfortunate because it gave Mrs. Angotti a chance to take a deep breath and then she was off again.

"I did, and a good thing, too, since you were saying it's some sort of disease and lots of people are already talking about taking their horses elsewhere, though what they'll do now they know it's a freak of nature and not a disease, I don't really know. But that's certainly better than something communicable, if you ask me. But I don't know what everyone else will say."

Mom and Dr. Herks and Martha all said together, "Who else knows?"

That was easy.

Mrs. Angotti knew.

And if Mrs. Angotti knew, everyone at the barn knew. She's what my mom calls a force of nature. A big whirlwind, I suppose. Or a geyser of hot water. Or a tsunami, which is a Japanese tidal wave that swamps an entire coastline.

"Everyone knows!" Mrs. Angotti confirmed, in the shortest sentence I have ever heard her utter. Or maybe it was short because no sooner was it out of her mouth then we all jumped up from the table and raced out to the barn, leaving her standing in the kitchen still holding on to Joey's arm.

There was no one cleaning stalls or wiping down horses or working on tack. There was no one going around in endless circles in the yard. Horses were tied up every which way, abandoned by their riders.

Everyone knew, all right! And everyone was standing at the open stall door, gaping. They were muttering too, using words like *monster* and *defective* and *abnormal*.

Agora, ears back, teeth showing, was straddling her colt. And he, poor baby, was sobbing uncontrollably for the first time in the short week of his life.

Mom and Dr. Herks waded into the crowd. Mom

shoved people aside, saying, "Move it, you big lump! Haul it over." And other even more descriptive terms about some of the gawkers. None of which was going to help us keep them as paying customers, but I don't think she was thinking about that at the moment. She just wanted to get in and comfort that little boy. Who happened to be part pony as well.

And Dr. Herks was just as angry. You don't want to get a Gulf War Vet angry — trust me. Even if he is a pacifist now.

Martha actually pushed Angela Angotti to the ground, though it wasn't on purpose, as she was herself shoved from behind. Which got Angela to screaming as if she'd been murdered. She has her mother's lungs.

I took the low route, crawling on my hands and knees till I'd crawled right into the stall. Agora recognized me at once and let me in. I put my arms around the centaur and petted him and sang in his ear until, like any toddler, he got distracted and began to smile.

It wasn't actually all that hard. After all, I had had a few weeks of being a sister. Everyone who was watching cheered, which set Agora off again. But the centaur seemed to think it was part of the game and clapped his hands.

Or almost clapped them. It was going to be another week before he quite got that right.

Mom suddenly got everyone's attention by shouting: "Come into the office and I'll explain everything."

And thinking there was more to know than what they could see, everyone followed her.

Martha whispered to me, "You stay here and watch Agora and her colt boy for me while I help your mother feed the multitudes." And when I nodded, glad to be out of the crowd, she left too.

Agora was still trembling and it was a long time before her ears came forward again. But the centaur boy was fine. He and I played peekaboo and Eensy Weensy Spider and then I taught him patty-cake. It was after the fifth recitation of patty-cake that I realized I couldn't keep saying, "Put it in the oven for baby and me." He was too big for a baby anyway. He needed a name.

"So what should we call you?" I asked.

"Goo," he said. Which I took to mean "Goo." "Pa-ca," he said. Meaning "patty-cake." No answer at all. But then he wasn't ready for a real conversation yet.

"Your mom is Agora. And other people think your dad is a Suss stallion, though I can't think why. Still, the way horses are named, it's usually a combination of their two names and I can't come up with anything using them that doesn't sound silly. Aguss is too much like a big bird. And Sugora is awfully like a cactus. So maybe I'll just call you . . ." I hesitated. But the name was right there on my tongue. We had used it before. Why not use it now?

"Bobby," I said. "Do you like it?"

He giggled and I pointed at him and said, "Bobby!" several more times. When he didn't object, I knew it would be all right. Especially when he pointed at his nose and said "Ba-ba."

I told him some horse nursery rhymes then, like "Ride a cock horse to Banbury Cross" and "Trot, trot to Boston." Afterward we played patty-cake over and over until his eyes began to go half-mast and at last he fell asleep, standing up, something humans can't do but horses can.

"He's all yours now," I said to Agora. But he had been hers from the first. Unlike the humans who had looked at him funny and had said words like *freak* and *impossibility*, Agora had never shied away from him. Not once. When I left, she was nuzzling him. His thumb and forefinger were both jammed into his mouth and he leaned against Agora as he slept, but didn't wake up. It had been a rough day for a baby.

It was a rough day for us as well. Mom had gotten everyone to promise not to say a word so as to give the little guy time to grow. She believed their promises.

But as I walked Dr. Herks to his car, he said, "Your mother is one of the world's innocents, Arianne." The furrows in his forehead were deeper than before, but for the first time I noticed how blue-gray his eyes were in the light.

"You don't believe them," I said, which was not a

question but a confirmation. And not a Quakerly thought at all. We are supposed to look for the good in people. "I don't believe them either."

"Oh, I believe they were sincere in promising," Dr. Herks said, "but that won't stop someone from spilling the beans. Which will hurt the little guy."

"Bobby," I said. "His name is Bobby."

"Bobby." He gave that half smile but that was because it was just an ordinary name to him. Then he paused and looked away from me for a moment. "It'll hurt Hannah too." The way he said my Mom's name — Hannah — confirmed my suspicions. It was kind of prayerful and soft. Then he looked down and those blue eyes were steel ball bearings. "You call me if anything happens and I'll be back like a shot."

It wasn't a very Quakerly thing to say. It was more a Vet kind of thing. Which was okay by me.

"I'll call just to tell you what's going on," I promised. And we shook hands like friends — not Friends — before a battle.

People were scattering to their various cars. No one, it seemed, was quite up to another ride or lesson or even to currying their horses. I had a lot of extra work to do that afternoon tidying up after them all.

By the time I was done, I was too tired for homework, almost too tired for bed, falling asleep in front of the television. Mom said she would have carried me upstairs if I'd been smaller.

That night I dreamed about geese flying over the farm and each one had the head of my dad on its shoulders.

The next day, first thing in the morning, even before the school bus got to the farm, there was a phone call. Mom answered it by saying, "Yes, yes, no and where did you hear about . . . well, you're wrong!"

She slammed the phone down and it rang again before she had time to take her hand away.

I didn't go to school that day but took turns answering the calls. In between, I called Dr. Herks and Martha and they arrived almost simultaneously. Martha listened for a minute to one of the calls, then hotfooted it out to the barn.

"I'll stand watch out there!" she called over her shoulder before she disappeared.

Dr. Herks just stood awkwardly, shifting from one foot to the other. The phone rang with another five callers. The fifth call had Mom in tears. Gently Dr. Herks reached over and took the entire phone, base and all, from her and unplugged it.

"No one says you have to answer, Hannah. But if you find it impossible to let it ring, we'll just turn it off."

"Thank you, Gerry," she said. Then she looked up at

the ceiling, tears still glistening in her eyes. "But they promised not to tell . . ."

Dr. Herks looked over at me and nodded and I ran over, put my arms around Mom, and said, "They meant the promise at the time, Mom, but that doesn't mean they could keep it. They just . . ."

"Yeah. I guess." She wiped her eyes. "Lack of sleep does not help."

The three of us walked out to the barn.

Martha had Agora and the colt in the enclosed arena and he was frisking around, waving his chubby little arms and calling out at the same time, "Baba. Baba."

We watched for quite a while, then Mom turned to me. "What is he saying?"

"His name."

"What name?"

I smiled tentatively. "I gave him a name yesterday. Couldn't just keep calling him You or Centaur or Whatever."

She nodded. "I expect you're right. But what kind of a name is Baba? Like Ali Baba?"

"Well, actually," I said, suddenly certain I had done the unthinkable. I stopped and took a deep breath.

Dr. Herks said, "Bobby. She's named him Bobby. And he can already say it."

There was a long silence. Longer than anything I could

ever have imagined. Long and deep and horrible. Then Mom turned and walked out of the barn.

Dr. Herks looked after her. "What was that all about?" he asked at last.

At first I wasn't going to say anything. It was a family matter, after all. And Dr. Herks wasn't family. But then Bobby saw me and cantered over, held out his arms and cried, "Ah-ah." I gave him a hug and then turned to see Dr. Herks staring at me.

"Are you going to tell me?" he asked. "Or do I have to ask your mother?"

I took a deep breath. "I had a baby brother," I said. "When I was five. He had lots wrong with him and he never got to leave the hospital."

"And his name was Bobby," Dr. Herks said, not a question.

I nodded. "He was one big birth defect," I whispered.

"That's a horrible thing to say. I am surprised at you, Arianne."

"That's not me speaking. My dad said that before he left for good." I held Bobby even closer and he began to squirm, so I opened my arms and he trotted away. "We never forgave him."

"I see," Dr. Herks said. And I believe he did.

Just then there was this horrible commotion outside and Dr. Herks and Martha and I ran out. There were three cars outside, none I recognized, and someone with a video camera on his shoulders marching purposefully toward the barn. Mom was trying to argue with him and he kept on coming, pushing by her as if she didn't exist. So Dr. Herks ran up to him, pulled his fist back, and was about to deck the guy when Mom shouted, "Gerry!"

Dr. Herks kept his fist up but made no more moves toward violence. He simply said, "I'd advise you to leave the premises before we call the police. You are trespassing and that's a felony."

I wondered suddenly if that was true or if it was something he had made up on the spot, like the centaur disease.

But it was too late to find out because someone from one of the other cars had evidently gone behind the house and then into the barn through a back door. He came out the front door with a stunned expression on his face. An expression that clearly said "Jeeze!" though what he actually said is part of a list of words I am not allowed to say in front of the paying customers.

After that, it was going to be CNN, Oprah, and all the rest. I mean, we couldn't have stopped it if we tried.

Except we did.

Sort of.

Dr. Herks and Martha and Mom and I had a quick conference while the photographers were inside taking their pictures.

Dr. Herks said, "Make lemonade, Hannah."

And when I asked what that meant, he said, "Something my mom used to say. 'When handed lemons, make lemonade.'"

I laughed, which was a funny sound at the moment. They all turned to me.

"Bobby," I said. "Birth defects," I said.

Mom looked angry and hurt and startled all at once. Martha's face was puzzled and she actually looked right at me. But Dr. Herks grinned. The first real grin I think I had ever seen him make.

When the reporters came out, Dr. Herks took over the interview. He told them that Mrs. Meyers — that's Mom — and Martha and I were going to homeschool Bobby and at the same time teach him to work with children with disabilities. "When handicapped children get on a horse," he said, "they're above the crowd literally. They will use muscles they've never used before because they aren't leaning against the back of a wheelchair or on a pair of crutches. And what better mount for them than a centaur who can talk with them and encourage them as they ride?"

The reporters ate it up, of course.

Mom smiled, and never more so than when the reporters talked to me.

"We're going to call it the Bobby Meyers Therapeutic Riding Association," I said. "After my baby brother who died of multiple birth defects when he was two weeks old."

Oprah did a whole show on us, shooting lots of footage at the farm. At the studio, Bobby played patty-cake with Oprah and said the alphabet. He spelled his name on the floor with his right forehoof. He pranced and danced and sang "Eensy Weensy Spider" with only a little prompting. And he didn't make a mess on the floor, which was a blessing indeed.

When she asked how soon he'd be working with children who had disabilities, he looked over at me because it was too hard a word for him yet.

"Not till he's two," I said. "In horse years that is. We think he'll be about fifteen then as a human. Older than me!"

Everyone applauded at that, and the noise startled him. But he didn't do more than roll his eyes. I stood with my arm around him and he quieted right down. He was terrific.

Back at the farm Mom gave him carrot cake in celebration and it became his favorite thing ever.

But even Oprah didn't get to see Bobby at his very best. That came a year later when he first carried Robin, my new and healthy baby brother, around the field.

Mom and Gerry watched from the door of the barn, arms around each other, their eyes shining with love.

And by Bobby's side, holding on to Robin carefully, I sang "Trot, trot to Boston . . ." a combination of lullaby and sister song to them both. And Bobby joined in with a shaky harmony, his voice cracking only on the highest note.

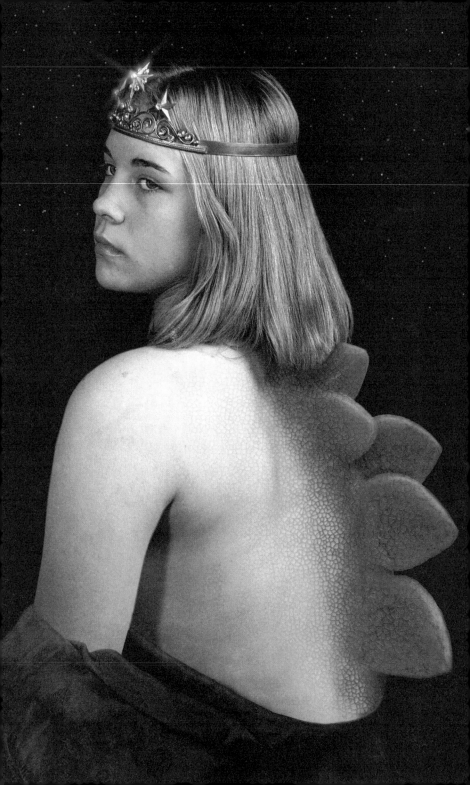

princess dragonblood

JUDE MANDELL

A long time ago, there was born to the aging king and queen of Morvetania, their first and only child, an infant of exceedingly strong will and unusual abilities. From the moment Princess Eleanor's forceful birth cry shook the summer breeze, it was clear she was different from most well-born baby girls.

"How wonderful, my queen!" said old King Rolf, as the nurse led him into the birthing room. "A child of our own, at last."

The exhausted queen lay with closed eyes. "Is she truly healthy?" she asked, in a voice of quiet dread. "The midwives say she is, but then . . . *why* will they not bring her to me to hold?"

"You are far too weak, my dear," said the king, stroking her gray hair. He went to the ebony cradle, knelt, and unwrapped the princess's swaddling clothes. He examined her from tip to toe in the flickering firelight, then held her up. "See for yourself," he said with satisfaction. "She is perfectly formed."

Queen Margot sank back into the silken pillows, the worry lines easing from her face. "Thank the Heavens," she whispered under her breath. "Perhaps it will come out right after all."

King Rolf propped the baby on his potbelly. "We shall call her Eleanor, after my great-grandmother."

Princess Eleanor gave a deep-throated chuckle, and reached out a plump fist toward the king, grasping the hilt of his sword.

"Cheeky creature," he said with a smile. "Let go!"

The baby clutched at the jeweled hilt, now with both hands.

"You'd think she knew the value of gold and emeralds already," said the king with a laugh that shook his white beard. He tried to pry off Eleanor's stubborn fingers. "How strong she is!"

A green flame of pride scampered in the depths of the princess's eyes. She gave a soft gurgle and smiled.

"Oh, she will slay hearts, this one," said the king delightedly. "No prince who sees her will be safe. Nor will his sword, for that matter." With a final tug, he yanked the hilt free.

Though Eleanor screeched with outrage, she managed to retain two gold-encrusted emeralds nonetheless.

"What a voice!" the king cried, thrusting the bawling babe at the waiting wet nurse. "Take care her shrieks don't curdle your milk, my good woman!" Hands clapped to his ears, he hastened to Queen Margot's bedside, gave her a hurried kiss, and then bolted out the door.

As the queen watched her hungry, blond daughter suckle at the wet nurse's breast, she tried to quell the fear that lurked beneath her joy. She had tried for years to conceive a baby, to no avail. Year after year passed, until she reached the age of graying hair and wrinkles, when it is almost impossible for a woman to bear children. Desperate, she and the king sent a royal proclamation to the far reaches of the kingdom and beyond, promising great riches for any barber-surgeon who could guarantee them a healthy babe.

Though many came forward, none succeeded. As the days passed, the queen and king resigned themselves to whatever the Fates would bring. But it was not the Fates who eventually took a hand. It was the queen herself.

Remembering, Queen Margot drew her ermine coverlet closer, as though a sudden chill had entered the stone-walled chamber. Her thoughts flew back to the note she'd sent secretly, months before, to a tumbledown cottage deep in the woods beyond the castle — a cottage known to harbor a woman who dabbled in magic.

Within hours, as if out of nowhere, an answering letter had appeared on the green velvet seat of the queen's throne. It was addressed, "For Her Majesty Only."

The yellowed parchment of the letter was bordered with mystical runes. Equally unsettling was the silvery ink that disappeared when struck by sunlight. Heart hammering, the queen hid the note in her sleeve so the king would not see it.

That night, when he was asleep, she read it by the moonlight streaming through the mullioned windows. Moments later, she donned her cloak and crept from the castle, stealing into the inky woods.

An avenue of thorn bushes led up to the witch's threshold. The oaken door creaked open before the queen could knock. "Come in, come in, Majesty," said the witch Glendora in cracked tones. A sly smile cut deep creases in her wrinkled, liver-spotted skin. Her eyes, sunken and dark, shone with a crafty light.

The queen entered, hesitant. "Your letter said you could ensure that I bear the king a child," she whispered. From beneath her jeweled cloak she took a delicately carved ivory box, placed it on a table, and opened the lid. Gold glinted. "Have I brought enough?"

Glendora's gnarled fingers fondled the coins. "The price is high for a barren queen wishing to bear a babe. This will do for a start — along with that diamond-studded cloak on your shoulders."

Queen Margot snatched off her cape. "It is yours. What else?"

The witch stroked the glittering garment with a rough palm. "Each year, on the child's birthday, you will give me double the gold in that casket. And, when I ask for it, you will send me your favorite jewel. In return I'll ensure you a healthy babe."

"What care I for gold or gems, compared to a child of my own?" cried the queen. "I will honor your bargain. You have my word."

Cackling softly, the witch nodded, seating the queen by the blazing hearth. She took an earthen jug decorated with scales from upon a rickety shelf covered with cobwebs. The jug was heavy. When the sorceress grasped its dragon-shaped handle, it glowed. Instantly, the smell of her burning flesh bit the air. Glendora did not flinch. With blistered hands she took a silver goblet, unstopped the jug, and poured a blood-red liquid into it. The metal tumbler smoldered, as if it contained fire. It hissed softly, steam rising from its lip. "Come. Drink," said the witch, holding it out. "This can give you your heart's desire."

The queen shuddered. She sensed the old woman's wickedness simmering like the liquid in the goblet, but her desire for a child was so strong it overcame any qualms. "To my child," she said, as if already toasting the happy event.

Throwing her head back, she drank deeply. A trail of fire coursed down her throat. Flames shot through her veins, her skin, to the very ends of her hair. She placed a hand on her belly, felt it quiver as the child formed within it. Moments later the babe stirred, then gave a healthy kick.

The half-empty goblet teetered when Queen Margot

set it down. In its reflection, she caught sight of her face now magically unlined, framed by hair no longer gray, but bright as spun gold. Feeling the child move again, she laughed, the tears streaming. "Thank you, thank you, my good woman! You have brought me such joy!"

Glendora stared at the queen's changed appearance as if awestruck, then snatched up the steaming goblet and gazed thirstily into its depths. "Your child will be as beautiful as you have become tonight, my queen. A jewel of a girl."

"A jewel indeed," cried the queen, light-headed from the drink and wandering in her wits. "My favorite jewel in the world!"

No sooner had the words left her mouth when she realized what she had done. She clutched at the table behind her for support.

"So it shall be!" crowed Glendora. "I have your word of honor. On her thirteenth birthday, you must send your favorite jewel, *your daughter*, to me. She will be the light of your life, an unusual child who will take after her warrior father in more ways than her strength and iron will."

"Her warrior father? You're mistaken. My husband, the king, is a man of peace."

The sorceress gave a cruel laugh. "Who said aught about your weakling husband? Your daughter will take after her *true* father, the cruel and powerful Dracon,

King of the Dragons." She brandished the goblet. "His blood has given her life!"

The queen put a hand to her throat. "It was Dracon's blood I drank?"

"Indeed. It surges through your child's veins even now." Glendora grinned. "One day, I shall present Princess Dragonblood to her father and reap a treasure in return. He'll transform her into a full-fledged dragon and keep her for company in his old age."

Queen Margot shook her head back and forth in denial. "No," she moaned. "No!" Then she crumpled unconscious to the floor.

She awoke back in her own chamber, with no memory of how she'd managed to find her way home. She hastened to the mirror. The dragonblood gold of her hair had grayed. Wrinkles once more creased her skin.

Seeing this, the queen hoped with half her heart the encounter with Glendora had been a dream. But then the child within her kicked, and with a thrill of joy, she knew with her heart's other half that it had been no dream. "Sleep, little one," she crooned, caressing the moving form. "I will care for you, come what may. As for the witch and her plans, we shall see what will be."

The next morning, she sent soldiers to bring Glendora in secret to the castle. Perhaps the sorceress would take some other reward than the cruel one she'd demanded the night before.

Hours later, one of the soldiers burst into the room with the news that Glendora's cottage had burned to the ground. Bones were strewn in the ashes, and a human skull.

Queen Margot felt a thrill of hope. Perhaps the witch was dead!

Now, gazing at her newborn infant, the queen prayed for such a miracle. "We will have you christened at once," she murmured to the sleeping baby. "May the blessings of the priests protect you from the witch's curse."

As the months passed, she waited anxiously to hear from the witch, demanding the next payment of gold.

No word came that year.

Or any year thereafter.

The queen finally rejoiced. Her daughter, Eleanor, was safe!

Princess Eleanor grew by leaps and bounds. Indeed, despite her parents' protests, she leapt and bounded about with the young squires all day. Mama might bemoan the fact that her only daughter had no interest in the domestic arts of spinning and needlepoint, but Eleanor just couldn't spare the time. She was too busy hunting and hawking and jousting in tourneys.

Through the age of nine, she thought herself as ordinary as the next princess. But when she turned ten, Eleanor began to notice subtle changes. She found herself stuffing her mattress with hoarded jewels and gold, and she was unable to sleep unless lying upon these treasures. She developed a fondness for food cooked so hot 'twould scorch an ordinary person's tongue. As if that were not enough, she began sprinkling hot pepper on everything edible. To compensate, she took to eating vast quantities of ice cream, saying jokingly, "It quenches the fires within me."

After her eleventh birthday, when more changes followed, Eleanor joked about such traits no longer. Her singing voice began to rasp and roar, with a curious hiss now and then, like escaping steam. She resorted to mouthing the hymns in church, so no one would notice.

Her fingernails and toenails grew remarkably fast, acquiring a pearly coating that shone in sunlight. If she did not clip them daily, they curved repulsively, like talons.

She began having tantrums, whipping the trailing hem of her surcoat back and forth, as if it were a tail. She hastened to make amends for these unwelcome mood shifts. Papa kissed her for her efforts, but Mama was clearly disturbed by these fits of temper, as was Eleanor herself.

The day of her twelfth birthday, while bathing, Eleanor detected a queer set of bulges running down the ridge of her back and upon her shoulder blades, as though something loathsome and foreign was lurking beneath the skin. She dismissed her maid and ran, wet and trembling, to her mother, lowering her robe to reveal this latest discovery.

Breathless, Queen Margot tried to convince Eleanor that these bizarre alterations were common to every growing girl. But Eleanor could tell that her mother was as frightened by the changes as she was herself, and was not reassured.

To keep from worrying, Eleanor threw herself into mastering the arts of war. She so distinguished herself, her father gave in to her request and knighted her, despite the protest of the holy priests, who said this honor should be reserved for men only.

"And Papa," she coaxed, "'tis not uncommon for the lady of the castle to guide the estate's defense in the absence of the lord. Since you have no taste for warlike pursuits and Mama avoids the very mention of blood, the task should fall to me."

The king, ill and bedridden, agreed. And so, the princess began rigorously training the castle's company of knights, squires, and men-at-arms. They chafed at being under a woman's command, but as their skills and pride increased, they saw in her the gift of leadership. She swore them to fealty and won their hearts as well.

On the morning of Eleanor's thirteenth birthday, her father fell into a stupor and could not be awakened. At dusk, another letter mysteriously appeared on the cushion of the queen's throne.

Queen,

The day of reckoning has arrived. I will come
to the castle tomorrow at daybreak to take what
is rightfully mine. Ready the twelve yearly pay-
ments of gold you owe, as well as the jewel we
agreed upon. You thought to cheat me, didn't
you, sending your soldiers to capture me the
morning after we struck our bargain? Well,
now that I have built up an army of my own to
ensure my safety, I come to claim my reward.

Glendora

Eleanor watched her mother's face age, reading the note.
Plucking the missive from the queen's shaking hand,
Eleanor read it through herself. She looked up, puzzled.
"I don't understand, Mama. Who is this person? What
bargain does she mean?"

In a voice as still as death, the queen told her daughter
of the pact with the witch.

Eleanor's knees turned liquid with shock. Staring at
her mother, she groped for an iron ring fastened to the
wall, to keep herself from falling. "And all these years you
let me believe I was normal, Mama? How could you?
When you *knew* I was a monster."

"You are no monster!" cried Queen Margot. "No
matter what effect the dragon's blood has had on you, you

are far more human than dragon. I thought you were safe, child. That the witch was dead. Now I must keep my word, and give you to her tomorrow. Though my heart will surely die if I do."

Eleanor firmed her quivering lips. "Neither you nor the witch consulted me about becoming a dragon or a dragon's companion for the rest of my days. I refuse to be bound by your bargain."

"But the sorceress has troops!"

Eleanor bristled. "Does she? Well, so do I, and rather well-trained troops at that, for I trained them myself! I will go to meet this Glendora, Mama. Your oath of honor demands it. But I intend to fight whomever I must to be free and human, be it witch, dragon, or both!"

The sun was just poking over the mountains the next morning, when Eleanor went to bid her parents good-bye.

King Rolf lay on the bed, unable to move, cheeks pale as parchment. Eleanor bent and kissed him.

The queen was already up and dressing. "Eleanor, I am going with you, to protect you as best I can. Were it not for my folly, you would not be in this predicament."

"But, Mama, think of Papa. He needs your loving hand to help him recover. And it would make my task harder having to watch out for you."

The king moaned. Queen Margot glanced at him worriedly. After a moment, her hands reached to her neck, to the locket that always hung there, her tiny portrait painted on its face. "Take this, then, Eleanor. It was given to me by your father. When you touch it, its magic will convey to you my love and support."

Hot tears filled Eleanor's eyes. "I will make good use of it. Come with me as far as the drawbridge, Mama. We will say our good-byes there."

A brigade of Glendora's troops waited at attention just beyond the moat. There were at least two hundred of them, astride horses and on foot, all goblins, their weapons at the ready. Eleanor eyed them guardedly. Were these fierce creatures as skilled as her own warriors, who, on her orders, now waited in secret ambush on the road to Dracon's lair?

A beautiful woman glided forward, riding a broom made of straw and twigs. She was cloaked in a queenly black cape, blazing with diamonds. A slender wand in a thin leather scabbard poked above her left shoulder. Eleanor studied the wand. Wielded skillfully, its magic could turn the tide of battle in the witch's favor.

"Glendora?" said Queen Margot, in a voice full of doubt.

"Yes, Majesty, 'tis I. Made lovely by dragon's blood, like you. Your looks have faded — the price for creating a new life, I suppose." The sorceress smoothed the cascade of her black hair. "Dracon's blood gave you your heart's desire: a child. I desired something different. I drained the cup and burst into flames! I rose from the ashes childless — but forever lovely."

She turned to Eleanor with a cruel laugh. "You will experience a harsher change, my dear. Imagine how you'll look once Dracon burns away your beauty with his fiery breath, revealing the hideous dragon beneath."

Eleanor shuddered, her mouth dry. "Do not worry," she murmured to her mother, who shook with sobs, "I'll return to you and Papa safe and sound. I promise."

Her words seemed to calm the queen. She grabbed Eleanor's hands and pulled her close. "No matter what happens, remember that you are human, above all. If you are tempted to give in to the dragon inside you, resist with all your might, or it will overpower you, and you will become the monster you fear."

As Eleanor moved off, flanked by two goblin soldiers, she took one last glance at the castle, all she knew and loved dissolving in a haze of tears.

"I am surprised you came so obediently, Princess," remarked Glendora, hovering on her broom in the air above. "Being Dracon's daughter, I'd have sooner expected you to kill me."

"Did you never think I might wish to meet this father of mine?" Eleanor asked. "He gave me the gift of life after all, among *other*, shall we say . . . gifts? I wish to pay him back."

Glendora glanced at Eleanor's curved fingernails, pearly in the sunlight, and smirked. "With a sword thrust to the heart, no doubt!"

After a full day's journey, they reached the East Woods, at the foot of Mount Drag. They had just passed the last thicket of trees, when Eleanor shouted, "To arms, my men, to arms!"

Out of the branches came a barrage of white-tipped arrows as her hidden soldiers shot crossbows from the trees. Goblins fell around her like threshed wheat. With a cry of rage, the witch glared at Eleanor. "You little monster. I should have expected this!"

"You should have expected *this* too," said Eleanor, spinning the sorceress about, knocking her flat, and snatching the magic wand from its scabbard. With a sharp crack, she broke the wand in half.

Glendora got to her feet, broom in hand, screeching with fury. Eleanor seized the broadsword of the nearest dead goblin, and aimed straight for the witch's heart. But at that moment, a burly goblin leapt onto Eleanor's back, knocking her off balance. She toppled over, then leapt up again, sword in hand. A thrust or two of her blade, and her attacker fell dead, his rotted teeth bared in spite.

She looked about for Glendora. But by this time the witch was flying above the battleground on her broom, speeding in the direction of Mount Drag. "We will meet again, Princess," Glendora called back to her with a venomous look. "You may count on it."

The battle raged for hours.

When Glendora's army had finally surrendered, and the surviving goblins had fled, Eleanor bandaged the bleeding wound on her wrist, then raised her gaze toward the mountaintop, wreathed in clouds. She pictured Dracon up there, coiled in his lair, waiting to claim her future. "The next battle," she murmured, "will be between us, my father . . . my enemy. You may count on that."

Bidding her troops to return home, Eleanor began the lonely trek up the treacherous cliffs of Mount Drag.

The mountain was well named, for her feet dragged heavier and heavier with each step.

Days passed. Now and again, the silhouette of a winged, lizardlike creature spread across her path, as if foreshadowing the horror of her destiny. It was then Eleanor would clutch the locket about her neck. Each time, Queen Margot's love flowed through her, a comforting balm, giving her the strength to continue on.

At last, skirting the open ground, she reached the place of Dracon's den. The cave was carved into the side of the mountain. Around it, the earth was scorched, littered with bones. Drawn by the boom of waves, and the ocean's salt tang, she peered over the cliff. Far below, restless whitecaps swirled atop a blue sea, fathoms deep.

Listening for the scrape of Dracon's scales, she stole toward the mouth of the cave. She heard nothing from inside it but a curious whine, high, sweet, and melodious. Cautiously, she entered. The den was empty of everything save a deep pit loaded with horrid, rotting bones, and Dracon's treasure trove. The glitter and shine of this lavish pile pulled her like a magnet. Being weary, she lay down upon it. The treasure hummed a lullaby, soothing her to sleep.

When she awoke, it took a moment or two to realize what had happened during her slumbers. The bulges on her back had swelled! Her nails, both hands and feet, had grown several inches in as many hours, and were already curving into claws! The breath flowing from her nose had grown so hot it singed her upper lip!

Eleanor's stomach turned over. At this rate, Dracon would have no need to *burn* her into dragonhood. She must get away!

But before she could move, a loud crackling noise intruded over the beat of her panicked heart. It had the sound huge wings might make, slapping upon the wind.

Dracon.

Eleanor had not expected such magnificence. Golden

scales, emerald eyes, and cruel teeth that shone like ivory. Mesmerized, she moved, inching along the rock face, closer and closer toward the cliff.

The smell of sulfur and brimstone oozing from Dracon's mouth flooded her senses, filling her with energy. The smell made her spine tingle deliciously and her shoulders itch. She leaned against a jagged ledge, rubbing her back against it to increase the sensation, her nostrils breathing in and out with pleasure.

And then Glendora's voice came floating to her on the wind. "We met years ago, you will recall, Sire."

Eleanor flinched.

"At the time, you gave me some of your heart's blood so I might get you a half-human child to care for you as you grow old. You promised to reward me for this boon."

"What an improvement in your appearance, Glendora!" Dracon interrupted in a low, rasping growl. "The last time I saw you, you were a crotchety old crone. How did you manage it?"

"That is neither here nor there, Sire," Glendora said.

"Dragon's blood, enough of it, could have done it," mused Dracon. "So you drank it yourself, did you? Wasted it to satisfy your vanity?" Dracon let out a sudden roar. Fire and smoke billowed.

"No, no, Sire!" protested Glendora in a terrified voice. "Because of me you have a daughter, Eleanor, your own Princess Dragonblood."

"You managed this feat without trickery?" asked Dracon. "The girl's parents will not claim her? She is mine, totally, as I insisted?"

"Er, in a manner of speaking. Sire, may I be so bold as to ask *why* you needed a half-human child? Would not your own dragon family care for you, if need be?"

Eleanor held her breath, waiting for the answer to the riddle of her birth.

Dracon threw his head back and roared with mirth, little spurts of flame shooting from his nostrils. "That soulless lot? They would be so busy squabbling over who would get my treasure when I died, they wouldn't notice if I did! I need someone with a tender heart and a hard head who will care for me, *and* guard my treasure. Now, where is she? Where is this daughter of mine?"

"Making her way here, Sire. Be on your guard! She is already rebelling against her dragon heritage. I suspect she'll stop at nothing to become fully human again."

"The witch tells the truth about *that*, at least," said Eleanor, striding from behind the rock face. "Take pity on me, Dracon. I am born of Glendora's treachery. Restore me to my human self, and let me return to the parents who love me."

"The parents who —" Dracon glared at Glendora, but she was already inching away. His massive head turned back to Eleanor. "My answer, Child, must be no. Accept your destiny." He swung round and glided toward the spot where Glendora had disappeared.

Desperation clutched at Eleanor. She ran at Dracon, sword raised. It came down hard on his scales, but glanced off with a loud, metallic clang.

He turned his head. "Enough," he said.

"Enough?" said Eleanor. "Are you so selfish you refuse to freely give your child that which would ensure her happiness?"

"We dragons are a selfish lot. It is our nature. We don't give up treasure willingly, especially a treasure such as you."

"I am not some nugget of gold, or bag of gems," Eleanor cried. "I am a person, more human than dragon. Fight me for my freedom, at least! Why will you not fight?"

His scales scraping the ground, Dracon stopped, then faced her once more. "Because I might hurt you," he said gently. "Why would I hurt the one thing in the world I love?"

Eleanor was as stunned at Dracon's words as she was to see that his eyes were full of tears. Her sword lowered.

Seeing her hesitation, Glendora darted forth from behind a huge boulder, grabbed the sword, and in a sudden movement, thrust it into the most vulnerable part of Dracon's body — the soft spot under his jaw.

Roaring with pain, Dracon writhed, his tail lashing like a powerful serpent, his wings trembling. He fell and his color began to fade, from bright gold to dull gray. A pool of steaming blood spread beneath him.

"You spiteful creature!" Eleanor cried. "If he dies, he can never change me back."

The witch looked amused. "Why should I give a fig for that? You heard him. He will never share his treasure with me. Once he is dead, I can take it all."

Weeping, Eleanor dropped to her knees beside the heaving dragon. His slitted eyes opened, their emerald sheen dulled. "Would that those tears were for me, Eleanor, and not for yourself," he rasped. "Then, perhaps, I might be saved."

The dragonblood in Eleanor's veins pulsed harder. "What can I do to help?" she asked. "Tell me." She had come here prepared to kill this dragon-father of hers. Yet, she sensed now that if she let him die, a vital part of her, the human part, would die an uglier sort of death.

He shook with pain, smoke oozing from his nostrils. "It will make no difference in your own condition, you know," he whispered. "I haven't the power to make you wholly human again."

"I understand," Eleanor said, pity for his torment overcoming her despair. "What must I do?"

"Press the wound on your wrist to my stab wound. Quickly! Without your lifeblood I will not live another hour."

She wondered for a heartbeat if his death might free

her from the dragon inside her. In the next breath, she thrust her wrist against his stab wound and felt their blood mingle.

A warm glow spread through her body.

"You fool!" shrieked the witch, watching the golden tinge return to Dracon's mottled skin. "You're bringing him back to life!" She leapt at the bleeding hulk, dagger in hand.

Eleanor grabbed Glendora's arm just in time. The two of them wrestled, rolling over and over. Each tumble brought them closer to the cliff's edge. The sorceress struggled, bit, pulled Eleanor's hair. Eleanor would not let go even after they fell over the precipice and hurtled down, splitting the waves in a fountain of foam, the knife plunging to the ocean floor.

Water closed over Eleanor's head. She felt pressure in her chest from the lack of air, yet still held Glendora fast. She would drown, but she would not drown alone.

"Let her go," echoed a voice in her mind. "Save yourself."

"No," answered her thoughts, "she will try to kill you again."

"Perhaps. But she will not succeed. Spread your wings!"

Glendora wrapped her fingers around the queen's locket, pulling it too tight for breath. Air bubbled from Eleanor's lips. "I have no wings, Dracon!"

"You do, Child, if you want them."

Eleanor recalled her mother's parting words: *No matter what happens, remember that you are human, above all. If you are tempted to give in to the dragon inside you, resist with all your might, or it will overpower you, and you will become the monster you fear.*

She closed her eyes, feeling her faintness growing. "If I die, Dracon, I will die trying to stay human."

"You *are* human, Child. And you are *dragon* too. Would you not rather be both than nothing at all? You must learn to love everything you are. Then you can choose what you wish to be."

The truth of his words echoed inside her. She gave a convulsive shudder, tightened her whole being, and pushed!

There was a tremendous ripping sound as the membranous wings on her back burst free. They flapped, thrusting her upward through the water. As she rose above the waves, the witch fell with a wail back into the sea.

Dracon, in a blaze of fire and smoke, flew to meet her, a magnificent creature, with golden scales, emerald eyes, and teeth that shone like ivory. Her father, who was no longer her enemy.

They alighted together upon the cliff top. "I cannot change what you are," Dracon said. "But I can show you how to manage the dragon part of you, so you can straddle both your worlds. We'll start at once. We can't have you going home looking like that."

"Go home? But . . . you said —"

He smiled ruefully. "That dragons never willfully give up their treasure? True. But you see, Eleanor, I am no longer wholly dragon. The blood you shared with me has seen to that." He eyed the queen's picture on the locket around her neck. "I am sure your parents wait anxiously for your return. Now, fold your wings back, extend your talons, and suck in your breath hard!"

Eleanor winced as the wings and talons retracted. She looked at him reproachfully. "You didn't warn me it would hurt."

"Patience. It will get easier. Now go along home."

Eleanor looked at him wistfully. There was a part of her that felt rooted here. "You'll let me go so easily, Father?"

"You are my heart's blood, Child," he said gently. "I've felt your presence in the World since the moment you were born. But I never understood until now that your happiness could mean more to me than my own."

"Are you *sure* you don't wish me to stay?"

"You are the daughter I dreamed of — filled with the fire and passion of dragons, tempered by the warmth and compassion of humans. I look forward to the years we will someday spend together. Until then, come visit me whenever the full moon lights the sky. I have much to teach you of dragon craft."

She reached out and stroked his muzzle. It was scaly and hard, but warm. "And I have much to teach *you* of humankind."

He chuckled. "Until the next full moon, then. It's my birthday, you know. We'll celebrate it together."

Eleanor smiled, her eyes misting. "What a lovely present for us both, Father." She started off down the hill, then turned back and threw him a kiss.

He blew one back, a tiny flame that hovered about her face for a moment, before hissing off into the blue, blue sky.

soaring

TIM WAGGONER

Icarus, dressed only in a pair of faded jeans, stood on a tree stump, facing into the wind, large gray wings spread out behind him. It was going to be different this time. It had to be.

He heard Mr. Bright's voice in his head. *Give 'er a try, boy! Spin the wheel, draw a card, toss a ring . . . what have you got to lose?*

He strained to spread his wings even wider, then tensed his legs and jumped. For an instant — a brief, glorious second or two — he hovered in the air. And then he was falling. Instinctively, he folded his wings against his back, put out his hands to catch himself, and angled his right shoulder so it would take the blow instead of wrists or elbows. He hit hard. He lay on his side, sucking breath between his teeth, shoulder throbbing. It wasn't fair, it just wasn't fair!

"You okay?"

Icarus looked up. A barefoot blond girl in a light blue dress came hurrying toward him, a worried look on her face.

"I guess," he said softly. "I don't think I broke anything."

Bethany reached down to help him up, but he ignored her outstretched hand and got to his feet on his own. He brushed off his jeans, resisting the urge to reach up and massage his bare shoulder. He didn't want her to know how much it hurt.

"I know I shouldn't have followed you," she said, not sounding apologetic in the slightest. "But when I saw you leave camp, I figured you could use some company." She nodded toward a grove of trees a dozen yards away. "I hid and watched you from over there."

"Did it ever occur to you that maybe I didn't *want* any company?" he snapped.

She smiled. "No."

He sighed. Bethany was the niece — and assistant — of Madame Mahalia, the resident fortune-teller of Bright's Traveling Phantasmagoria. And Bethany, like her aunt, placed great stock in intuition and hunches.

"C'mon," he said, "let's go back." He started walking in the direction of camp, Bethany keeping pace at his side. This portion of southwest Ohio was beautiful in midsummer: flowing green grass, bees drifting lazily from daisy to dandelion and back again. The warmth made it comfortable for him to go about shirtless — a condition he preferred so his wings didn't feel restricted.

They walked in silence for a few moments before she spoke. "Why did you decide to try again? I thought you gave up trying to fly after you broke your wrist last summer."

Icarus didn't want to answer, but he knew Bethany would just keep after him until he did.

"I've been having the dream again." He glanced at her sideways, scratching at the feathery gray down on his cheek with a finger that resembled a bird's claw. "You know, the one where I'm flying."

"How long have you had it this time?"

"A few weeks." She gave him a skeptical look and he said, "All right, two months."

"Why didn't you say something?"

He shrugged and his wings rustled. "I don't know. Maybe I didn't want you to lecture me again about the importance of dreams."

"Is there anything different about the dream this time?"

"Look, Beth, I really don't want to talk about it right now, okay?"

"Remember our deal? You don't call me Beth, and I don't call you Ick. Now quit trying to weasel out of this and tell me more. I can't help you interpret your dream if you won't talk about it."

Icarus wanted to groan. It annoyed him when she went into New Age Freud mode. But part of him wanted to tell her, wanted to hear what she had to say. Besides, they'd known each other all their lives, fifteen years. If he couldn't tell her, he couldn't tell anyone. "It's mostly the same. I'm flying above a lake, so close to the water that I can see my reflection. I'm a hawk. I feel the wind flowing around my body, so naturally and easily it's as if we were made for each other. And I feel so free, so . . ." He shook his head. "I don't have the words to describe it. Maybe there aren't any."

"It sounds more intense than it used to be."

"It is." Icarus had been having this same dream, or variations on it, his entire life. "Now, I'm not just a human being seeing the world from a hawk's point of view. I *am* a hawk. . . ."

"Icarus . . ." Bethany trailed off, as if she were determined to choose her words carefully. "You know you're never going to fly, right?"

He stopped walking. He thought of a time when they lay on the ground and looked up at the clouds, remembered Bethany saying, *I wonder when your wings will be big enough so you can fly?* "You used to believe I'd fly one day. At least, that's what you said."

"I *did* believe then." She thought for a moment. "I don't know. I guess I believed because you seemed to need me to so bad."

She reached out to touch him, but he drew away. "So what changed your mind?"

"Science," she said simply. "Humans — even with a pair of wings as big as yours — are too heavy to fly, and their bodies aren't shaped right."

Icarus laughed. "Ms. Psychic is talking to me about science?"

"That's different. Psychic stuff comes from the spirit. Flying is physics."

His hands tightened into fists. He could feel his sharp nails cutting into the flesh of his palms. "Why are you telling me this now?"

"Because someday you're gonna try something really stupid, like jumping out of a tree, or maybe off a cliff, or a water tower, and you're gonna get hurt. Maybe killed."

He sneered. "Is that a prediction from the great psychic?"

She shook her head. "I worry about you, you big dummy." She punched him on the arm, a little harder than necessary. "You're like . . . you know, the brother I never had."

"Oh yeah? Well, you're like the sister I *wish* I'd never had!" He took off running before she could reply, his long, nimble legs carrying him away from her with great, leaping strides. And when the tears began, he told himself they were caused by the wind blowing in his eyes.

Icarus's first show wasn't until after lunch. He picked up a lemonade at a juice joint, and went to his tiny trailer to eat alone. Along with his drink, he had a ham sandwich and an apple. Carny folk rarely ate the greasy, sugary muck that customers picked up at grab joints.

After lunch, Icarus went to his performance tent — his very own, a mark of distinction — and entered through a flap in the rear. Inside was a dais upon which rested a wooden stool. Icarus would've preferred a more comfortable chair, but he remembered Mr. Bright's advice.

You want to keep things as simple as possible, boy. An attraction should sell itself with the least amount of ornamentation possible. Besides, a stool looks a lot more like a bird perch than a La-Z-Boy does.

He mounted the dais, took his seat, and spent a few moments stretching his wings to limber them up. As the barker outside urged passersby to stop and see "the amazing wild bird-man," Icarus tried not to think about what Bethany had said to him, told himself to put her out of his mind and concentrate on his work. A minute later the dais began to rotate, the electric motor beneath it whirring softly. It was showtime.

Remember, people don't come just to see a winged boy, Mr. Bright used to tell him. *They come to see a show. So make sure you give it to them.*

As the people began filtering in, Icarus ruffled his feathers the slightest bit, cocked his head at a birdlike angle, fixed his gaze upon them, staring intently as if trying to size up whether they were threat or prey.

The onlookers were quiet at first. They usually were until the crowd became large enough to offer some anonymity. Then the whispering began.

"Do you think those wings are real?"

"I wonder when molting season starts?"

"Look at the way he jerks his head. He moves just like a bird!"

Then, a bit louder, "Why don't you lay an egg for us?"

Laughter, some nervous, some mean. The joke didn't bother Icarus. He'd heard it too many times before. But as always, he used it as a cue to flap his wings suddenly, once, twice, three times, whipping the humid air within the tent into a mini-hurricane. He let out a shrill, high-pitched hawk's cry that he'd worked for years to perfect. The laughter died instantly and the people drew back from the rotating dais, half-afraid, half-exhilarated at the sight of his wings actually working.

But then they didn't *really* work, did they? He had a wingspan of almost twelve feet, but they still weren't big enough. He could flap them all he wanted and they wouldn't bear him aloft, wouldn't help him escape the tyrannical grasp of gravity. Wouldn't help him *fly*.

Depressed, he folded his wings against his back and sat, elbow on knee, chin on fist, not bothering to act like a bird anymore. He just stared over the crowd's heads as he spun slowly around, a boy with useless wings.

He skipped his next two shows, telling the barker outside that he had a bad headache. He went back to his trailer, turned on the ancient air-conditioning unit, walked over to the bed, and flopped onto his stomach. He thought of the people who paid money to stand in the sweltering air of his tent to gawk at him.

He knew that some of them thought he was a freak, a mistake of nature that had no right to exist except as another curious attraction in Bright's Traveling Phantasmagoria. Just another carny geek. But Icarus didn't think of himself like that. He was special, one of kind. Mr. Bright had said so.

From the moment your mother brought you to us, a squalling infant, I knew you were a wonder, boy, a myth made flesh, an angel descended from the heavens to grace the dull existence of us mere mortals. To show us there's more to life than drudgery and tedium. To teach us how to wonder, to remind us how to dream.

Icarus knew the old man's words were as substantial as cotton candy, but they sure were sweet when he spoke them. He wished Mr. Bright were still alive. Until almost two years ago, Mr. Bright had been the only parent Icarus had known since his biological mother — whoever she was — had brought him to the carnival as a baby.

It was Mr. Bright who had given him the name of a figure in Greek myth: Icarus, a boy whose father created artificial wings so they both could fly. But the boy ignored his father's warnings not to soar too close to the sun, and his wings melted, sending the boy plunging to the ocean. In a way, Icarus envied his mythological namesake. At least that boy had known what it was like to fly, if only for a short time.

In his heart, he feared that Bethany was right, and that he was destined to be landbound forever, like a penguin or an ostrich. Sure, there were other ways to fly, or at least simulate flying — planes, hang gliding, skydiving. But none of them appealed to him. They would be at best second-rate substitutes for the actual thing.

No, he thought as he closed his eyes. *Better to stay on the ground and be miserable.*

Wings spread easy, gentle air molding to his body, over, under, around sleek contours, holding him high, almost motionless, save for minor corrections in altitude, a wing tilt here, a head lift there. Sun above, waves beneath, the wind and him, forever.

The silence of calm water, glitter-scatter of sunlight. Angle to the right, wingtip trails water, fine white line carved in glassy blue, spray jetting behind.

Dipping too low, wing dragging, water tugging, pulling, gathering him in, quick and hungry. One last flash of sky blue, then nothing but the weight and swirl of dark water.

"Wake up!"

Icarus opened his eyes. Bethany had hold of his shoulders and was shaking him. He waved her away and sat up groggily. "I'm okay now."

"You were yelling in your sleep. I could hear you all the way across camp."

As Icarus came more fully awake, he remembered the last words he had spoken to Bethany. "Uh, you know that stuff I said in the clearing . . . about how I wished you weren't my sister, I mean, weren't *like* my sister —"

"Forget it. I wasn't listening anyway." She smiled. "Tell me about your dream. It must have been pretty bad to make you yell like that."

Icarus told her.

"That ending's new, right? You never fell into the lake before."

"Yeah, it's new, but I was thinking about the Icarus of Greek myth just before I fell asleep, so maybe that got mixed into my dream."

Bethany looked doubtful. "Maybe. Maybe not." She seemed to come to a decision. "I think it's time I did a reading for you."

Icarus started to protest, but Bethany ignored him. She grabbed his arm, pulled him off the bed, and dragged him toward the trailer door. Icarus sighed. When Bethany was this determined, you had two choices: go along quietly, or go along complaining. Either way, you went along.

Icarus chose to go quietly.

✦　✦　✦

Madame Mahalia was with a customer, so they waited behind her tent until she was finished. While they could hear Mahalia and her customer talking in hushed tones, they couldn't make out specific words, which was fine with Icarus. He wasn't an eavesdropper.

They sat cross-legged and drank in the hurly-burly of the carnival going on around them. The lilt of calliope music, the shrill voices of barkers, the laughter of children. The mingled smells of cotton candy, hot dogs, straw, and sawdust. Kids begging their parents to give them a dollar so they could try their luck at a game of chance — pick a lucky number on a spinning wheel, toss a ring or a ball at a target — never knowing that the games were designed to be almost impossible to win, that they would end up getting "gaffed," or cheated, nearly every time.

Icarus found the tumult comforting. The carnival was the only home he had ever known, and he loved it.

After a bit, Mahalia finished with her customer, and Bethany hurried inside. Icarus couldn't hear exactly what she said to her aunt, but from their voices, he guessed Mahalia was lecturing her about responsibility and professionalism.

He was tempted to sneak off. Bethany had offered to do a reading for him many times over the years, but he had always refused. He wasn't sure why. He had told himself that it was because fortune-telling was just an act, so what was the point? But now, sitting behind Madame Mahalia's tent in the hot summer sun, he wondered if he had avoided having Bethany do a reading for him because he did believe in psychic powers — or at least hers — and he was afraid of what those powers might reveal.

Bethany came around the side of the tent. "My aunt's gone. I convinced her to take a lunch break since there were no customers waiting. Let's go."

Icarus wanted to tell her to forget it. Instead, he followed her around to the front of the tent and through the opening. Icarus had been inside many times over the years, but never for a reading. The first time he'd entered the tent, he'd expected wind chimes dangling from the ceiling, horoscope charts on the walls, a lamp with a gaudy fringed shade hanging over a table covered by a cloth decorated with half moons and suns.

He'd been disappointed to find that the tent looked rather ordinary. A round table with plain wooden chairs on opposite sides. A simple lamp, the kind that might rest on anyone's nightstand, sat atop a crimson table cloth. The only exotic touch was a pack of tarot cards stacked neatly on the table.

Bethany sat in one of the empty chairs and gestured for Icarus to take the other. He sat and said, "Now what?"

"First, I need to get ready." Bethany closed her eyes and began breathing slowly and deeply.

After a few minutes of watching her breathe, Icarus couldn't take the silence anymore. "Aren't you going to use the cards, or maybe look into a crystal?"

Bethany didn't open her eyes as she answered. "Those things are only props for show. You don't need them for a real reading."

"Oh."

Several more moments passed, and then Bethany said softly, "I'm ready." Keeping her eyes closed, she reached across the table. "Give me your hands."

Icarus hesitated. They had never held hands before.

"It'll help me do your reading. Besides," she added with a grin, "it's not like we're on a date or something."

Feeling self-conscious, Icarus placed his hands in hers. She held them lightly and her breathing became even slower and deeper.

At first he didn't feel anything, but after a bit his hands began to tingle, and he experienced a slight dizziness. But the sensation passed so quickly, he wasn't sure if it had been real or just his imagination.

Bethany released his hands and opened her eyes. She frowned.

"What's wrong?" he asked.

"Sometimes when I do readings, I get feelings about how to answer a customer's question or about what might happen to them in the future. But this time, words popped into my head, like someone whispered them to me. It was weird."

"Tell me."

"All right, but I don't think you're gonna like it. It's not real clear." She gazed at him intensely, her gray eyes seeming to sparkle with an internal light. "'Sometimes the only way to make a dream come true is to let it go.'"

Icarus waited, but Bethany said no more.

"That's it?" He was disappointed. Bethany's pronouncement sounded like a generic sentiment on a cheap greeting card.

"I don't like it either," she admitted. "Aunt Mahalia's always telling me I have a lot to learn about doing readings." She sighed. "I guess she's right. Sorry."

"That's okay. You did your best." He stood. "I think I'd like to be by myself for a little while. So I can think."

Bethany nodded. "I understand."

Icarus gave her a smile to show he wasn't upset about how the reading turned out, then left the tent. As he walked, he began thinking of dreams, and about giving them up.

Dusk found Icarus at the tree stump once more, though this time he sat looking toward the horizon, watching the soft orange-red of the sun sink behind the trees. He wasn't surprised when Bethany approached. She sat on the grass next to him and hugged her legs to her chest.

"I thought I'd find you here," she said.

"Looks like you thought right."

"You were gone for so long, I started to get worried. I'm sorry about the reading. I thought I could help."

"Maybe you did." Before Bethany could ask what Icarus meant, he said, "Why do you think I was born like this?" He rustled his wings.

"I don't know. I never really thought about it."

"I asked Mr. Bright about it once. He said I was a throwback to a time when human and animal spirits were closer than they are today. A time when centaurs, satyrs, and mermaids existed. I always figured he just made that up, but now I'm not so sure."

"I don't get it."

"What if people like me — half-human, half-animal — are that way because we don't just have one spirit inside us, but two? Twin souls, somehow trapped in one body."

"You mean like a human spirit *and* a bird spirit?"

Icarus nodded. "Most of the time the two spirits get along, but sometimes they need different things. A mermaid whose fish spirit longs for the ocean and keeps her underwater too long, until her human half drowns. A werewolf whose need to hunt finally causes him to take a human life."

"A bird-man who wants to fly," Bethany said softly.

Icarus nodded. "And that's what the bird spirit in me needs: to fly free."

"Now I know what your last dream meant!" Bethany

said suddenly. "When you fell into the water — that was your human half dragging the bird spirit down!"

"Yes, that's what I figured out too. And it always will. Unless I do what you told me." He stood and climbed upon the stump. "You said that sometimes the only way to make a dream come true was to let it go. That's what I have to do." He spread his wings wide to cup the humid summer breeze.

Bethany stood and took several wary steps backward. "I don't understand."

"To be honest, I don't either. But my bird self does." Icarus closed his eyes and heard Mr. Bright's voice one last time.

Spin the wheel, boy! Spin it hard!

Icarus spread his wings even wider, and let go.

He experienced a pulling, a tearing deep within; for a dizzying instant it felt as if he were two beings at once. And then he was left with a great emptiness, as if half his soul had fled, leaving a vast pit at the core of his being.

"Icarus! Look!" Bethany shouted.

He opened his eyes to behold a gray hawk rising into the sky. He looked down at his hands. They were pink, smooth, the fingers no longer like bird claws at all. He flexed his shoulder blades, felt no movement of wings, heard no rustle of feathers.

The hawk rose higher, circling above them. It let out a joyous cry that echoed through the hills.

Bethany came forward and took his hand. "You did it! You're flying!"

Icarus shook his head sadly. "No, he's flying!" He stepped off the stump, still holding Bethany's hand. They stood side by side and watched the hawk ascend farther into the sky.

Then, just as it looked as if the hawk might vanish into the clouds, it folded its wings against its body and dove toward them. Icarus felt the world tilt and suddenly he was looking down at a boy and girl holding hands, the girl in a blue dress, the boy wearing only a pair of jeans. He felt the wind whistling past him on all sides, sliding across his feathered body as if it were water and he a sleek torpedo of a fish. He opened his wings, slowed his dive, flapped against the air, and began gaining altitude once more. The sky was his, just as it was always meant to be. He was home.

Another tilt of the world, and Icarus was watching the hawk flap toward the horizon and the setting sun. The hawk cried out, and in his mind, Icarus heard a single word: *Good-bye*.

Icarus grinned as tears began to roll down his cheeks.

"Are you okay?" Bethany asked.

"Yeah," Icarus said. "We both are."

the hardest, kindest gift

BRUCE COVILLE

hree hundred years ago, when I was twelve, I sat
beside my father's deathbed in a stone cottage
near the west coast of France.

I knew that he was absurdly old. Even so, I could not
believe that he would really die — at least, not until I
heard the uncanny wailing outside the window, a heart-
piercing keening that seemed to twist and twine around
the house, seeping under the doors, through the shut-
ters, down the chimney.

My father started up in his bed, his face wild with fear
and longing.

"Mother!" he whispered.

Then he collapsed back against the pillow, his hand
clenching mine so tightly that I feared he might break my
fingers. He did not speak again for many hours — not
until the wailing had ceased, which did not happen until
the sun began to creep into the sky.

"I will be dead before nightfall," he whispered.

I flung myself across his chest, denying it, begging him
to stay, sobbing out my fear of being left alone.

I could not hold him to this world, of course, and by nightfall he was gone, just as he had predicted.

He left me three things: a fortune, a life that would be unnaturally long, and a story.

The story, which he told me during his last hour, laid hold of my imagination. In the end, it became the driving force in my life for the next two hundred years, for with it came a sense of obligation, and an awareness of a task I knew I alone was meant to perform.

The idea merely simmered inside me at first. Even when I began to see what I should do, I felt helpless, because I had no idea where to start. But the story continued to haunt me, as stories will, and at last the time came when I could put the task aside no longer.

So I began my search, which took me into stranger places than I ever would have guessed existed — including, eventually, a small, dusty shop called Le Grenouille Gris that I found on a side street in Paris.

Finding the shop was no accident. Fifteen years of dangerous questions and unlikely contacts had led me to a midnight-dark alley where a cold presence stood beside me like a shadow, whispered a hint, and then disappeared.

That hint was what led me to the shop.

Its proprietress was a gray-haired, gray-eyed, gray-skinned woman who looked as if she, like the items on her shelves, had not been dusted in many years.

"I'm looking for something special," I said.

She gestured toward the displays with that attitude peculiar to Parisian shopkeepers, who somehow seem to feel offended by your very presence in their stores. Without a word, she was clearly telling me, "Look if you must. But don't expect my help!"

Alas, her help was just what I needed, as I was fairly certain that the thing I sought was not on display. Risking a bolt of Parisian contempt, I refined my request. "It's something with wings."

I braced myself for her sneer. But the veiled hint had worked. I had at least caught her interest, and she bestirred herself to the point of actually gesturing toward one of the shelves. Turning, I saw a stuffed owl that looked as if it had once been left out in the rain.

It was not what I wanted, and she almost certainly knew it. But she was testing me.

I shook my head. "What I want would be smaller."

Her expression didn't change.

"And older."

Still no change.

I took my last, best shot, "And still alive."

Her eyes widened by the tiniest degree. In a voice that sounded like the rustle of dry grass in the autumn wind, she spoke the first words she had uttered since I entered: "What is your name?"

"Geoffroi LeGrandent," I said. Then, as if to defy the shame that even after all these years I was still not able to entirely hide, I added boldly, "The same as my father."

I saw the slightest flicker of surprise in those ancient gray eyes. She nodded and stood, so rickety and frail that I feared she might collapse before she could sell me what I wanted.

"Follow me," she wheezed, and shuffled off in a cloud of dust.

I made my way around the counter — not an easy passage, given the store's clutter. By the time I had picked a path between the bronze elephant and the display of cracked pottery, she had vanished behind a tattered gray curtain.

I hurried to catch up with her.

The room we entered was small, dingy, and even more cluttered than the store. A narrow bed — little more than a pallet covered by a thin blanket — stood tight against the far wall.

She pointed to it and said, "Under there."

I knelt. Beneath the bed was a wooden box — oak, I guessed — held shut with a padlock. I pulled it out, then, at a nod of her head, followed her back into the store, where I placed it on the counter.

The proprietress fumbled in her pocket, then drew forth a ring of keys. The smallest, needle thin and no longer than my thumbnail, opened the padlock.

I was scarcely able to contain my impatience at her

slow, deliberate movements. When she finally lifted the lid of the box I leaned forward eagerly. Inside was a single item, a glass cube, about four inches to a side.

Inside that vitrine prison, its ebony wings delicate as lace, fluttered the thing I had sought for so many years.

Far away, resting in her grotto, Melusine senses that something is happening. She doesn't know what it is, but she can feel it in her veins, the way she used to feel it when death was on the prowl for one of her family. But that was long ago. The bloodline is so thinned these days that she rarely feels that acid premonition, and then only as a faint, cold tingle.

But this is strong. When was it last this strong?

Shall I flee? *she wonders.*

No. It is not time for that. What has she to fear, anyway, save that which has already happened? And she does not want to leave her grotto, this sacred pool that is her shelter and her temple. Not yet. There is still time.

There is always time.

Much too much of it.

The moon rises.

She slides into the water to swim.

As I left Le Grenouille Gris with my prize, I thought of my father. How could I not, considering what I carried?

He had been a good man when I knew him. But in his youth he had been a beast. Oh, not in the literal sense. In fact, were my father's blood to be truly accounted he would, by some theories, be found one-half angel. Fallen angel, it is true. Yet he had his moments of grace. But it was the fallen part that so marked and marred his life, and drove him to the violent act that had the side effect of toppling the delicately balanced marriage of my grandparents into the realm of tragedy.

That was hundreds of years before I was born, of course. But, given the longevity I inherited from him, I have had time enough to piece together the story. The great key came with my discovery of my grandfather's testimony, moldering in the ruins of a fallen abbey — testimony that I alone have read in the last two hundred years.

Carrying my purchase, I left Paris that same night for the west of France, for the soil in which my family's strengths and sorrows have their root. As I traveled I read again the crumbling pages that held my grandfather's story.

Extract from the Testimony of Raymond de Lusignan, as offered to the Abbot of the Monastery of Saint Denis, in the year of Our Lord 953:

You have asked how I first met my wife. It happened because of what was, to that point, the worst day of my life. I had been hunting with my friend and protector, Count Aimeri of Poitiers. We had become separated when the count stumbled across an enormous boar. The boar attacked and managed to gore the count in the leg.

Attracted by my friend's scream, I raced into the clearing. When I saw what was happening I dashed forward, sword raised. But as I stood above them and slashed down, the boar and my dear friend twisted beneath me, changing places. The blade struck, and I cried out in horror as he who had been like a father to me died by my own hand.

Rage drove my sword again, and I dispatched the boar in a matter of seconds. Then I dropped to my knees beside the count and tried to staunch his wound. It was too deep. No matter how I pressed and held, I could not stop the flow of crimson life. Within moments he was dead.

Dropping my face into my bloodstained hands, I wept until I was senseless.

When I came to, I stumbled into the forest, feeling sickened by what I had done, stunned, and afraid for my very life if the accident should be thought murder when it was discovered.

In this sorry state I wandered aimlessly for several days.

Late one night, hungry, thirsty, and half mad, I came to a grotto, where I found three maidens dancing at the edge of a moon-silvered pool. The fairest of them came to me and asked what troubled me, and though I was afraid to confess what I had done, the words poured out of me like water from a jug.

She took my hands. They were still brown with the long dried blood of my uncle and looked strange lying in hers, which were white as milk. Then she led me into the pool, where she undressed me and bathed me, so that the blood and the sorrow and the fear all seemed to wash away together. I felt as if under an enchantment, and I suppose it is possible that I was, that she was working some spell on me. But I do not think that was the case. I think the only magic was the moonlight, and the pool, and her beauty, and her tenderness. I think the only magic was love, for I loved her then as I love her now, all these years and tears later, and would do anything to take back what happened.

Though several miles separated the train station from the stone cottage where my father had died, I made the journey on foot. I prefer walking when I have a great deal on my mind.

This was the first time I had been back since the night he died, and it seemed strange to see the old place again. I had kept it all these years, usually renting it for a pittance to some deserving family, but sometimes letting it sit empty with the vague thought that I would return to occupy it.

I never did, though whether that was because I had never been ready to settle down, or because I secretly feared it was haunted, I could not say.

The couple I had hired to take care of it had done their work tolerably well, and the dust was not too thick.

I slept fitfully that night, half expecting to hear a wailing at the windows.

When morning finally came I walked to what was left of my grandparents' castle, now not much more than some broken, moss-covered walls that bear mute testimony to its former grandeur.

The following morning I entered the woods. I carried a pack with enough food and water for three days, for I suspected that the way would be long, and that if I ate or drank anything in the place I was seeking I might never be allowed to leave.

Underneath those supplies, carefully wrapped to protect it, was the glass cube I had purchased at Le Grenouille Gris.

The trees were ancient, thick, gnarled. Their roots rumpled the leaf-covered ground and seemed to reach up to grab my feet as I passed, making my progress difficult.

Unseen creatures moved and muttered in the branches above me, in the undergrowth beside me. Mushrooms of an unnatural size, some a sickly blue-gray color, others a violent red, grew in clusters beneath the trees.

I carried a pad and made careful notes and sketches to help me remember my path. It seemed the best way, since I could not bring myself, in this forest, to use a hatchet to blaze a trail. I had considered bringing ribbons to tie around branches as markers, but I was fairly certain that when it was time to return I would have found the ribbons missing. Either that, or there would have been a hundred times more than I had originally brought, fluttering in bright profusion for the sake of my bafflement.

It comes closer. Melusine's heart flutters faster than her wings. Sorrow and memory, tangled together, rise like a flood and threaten to drown her.

What can it be? *she wonders, raising her head to the sky.* After all these years, what can it be?

As I made my way through the haunted forest my thoughts turned, naturally, to my father, and his great crime.

Like everything in our family, it had to do with family. His brother, in this case.

My father had nine brothers in all — nine uncles that I never knew, for each was dead before I entered this world. What I do know, both from my father and from the tales, is that each was stranger than the one who came before him, born with his own curse, and his own special gift.

Father was the seventh. He was named Geoffroi, but everyone called him Geoffroi-the-Tooth, or Geoffroi Big Tooth, or simply The Tooth because of the boarlike fang, bigger than a thumb, that jutted up from the side of his mouth. That was his curse, of course — that, and his temper.

The gift was his great strength. But that combination of strength and temper was a curse in itself, and he was both respected and feared in the lands surrounding my grandfather's castle.

Mostly feared.

One day my father and his younger brother, Froimond, got into a fight. No one knows, now, what it was about; some small thing that grew out of all proportion, probably. Fearful of his brother's temper, Froimond took refuge in a monastery.

My father, driven to a frenzy of rage at not being able to reach Froimond, started a fire at the gate that ended up burning the entire place to the ground. A hundred God-fearing men perished in that blaze — a hundred and one, if you count my uncle.

When word of this atrocity reached the castle, it drove my grandfather to speak the words that changed everything.

Memories crowd Melusine's mind more than usual tonight. As she gazes into the pool it seems she can see once more the face of her beloved Raymond as he was all those years ago.

How long since his death? How many centuries?

How long has she lived on in this loathsome shape, doomed by their mistakes, all their mistakes? How gladly would she lie in the earth at his side if she could.

She had loved him at once, first for his tender sorrow, his boylike confusion over the accidental killing of his friend Count Aimeri. Then, and more deeply, for the way he looked at her. Then, and most of all, for the unquestioning way that he accepted her demand that if they married she must be left to herself on Saturdays, and he must never question why.

No, *she thinks now.* Not my condition. The condition set upon me as punishment for my disloyalty.

Is it in my blood, *she wonders,* this flawed, imperfect nature? Is that what drove my poor Geoffroi when he committed his terrible crime — the blood he inherited from me, fallen angel that I am?

Then she wonders if this fault in the blood is why she herself is one of the Fallen. But what failed creator is this, who could not make his angels better beings?

EXTRACT FROM THE TESTIMONY OF RAYMOND DE LUSIGNAN, AS OFFERED TO THE ABBOT OF THE MONASTERY OF SAINT DENIS, IN THE YEAR OF OUR LORD 953:

The abbot asks if I didn't realize there was something strange about Melusine. Of course I knew she was different. How could I not? But I was so dazzled with love for her that I willingly accepted her condition for our marriage, that I must not seek to know what she did on Saturdays. Naturally this troubled me. But her love was so pure and strong that I set my concerns aside. When ever did mortal man have so beautiful a bride? And she brought to our marriage both wealth and cleverness, first guiding me as I made my peace with Count

Aimeri's family for his accidental death, then building our home.

And then the children.

Guy was the first, as you know. Guy with his startling eyes, one green as the forest, one red as blood. Then his brothers, each with his own deformity and his own gift. At first, love blinded me to their oddities — love for the boys, love for their mother.

Of course the whispering began, the dark rumors that Melusine had a secret lover, that our children carried demon blood. You know how the peasants talk. Yet most of that I did not hear. And in the six days we had together every week Melusine was so tender and so true, so attentive to me, to the boys, that I could not doubt her love.

She used to sing to me at night, you know, her voice like the clear sound of a mountain stream.

I think that's what I miss most of all. Her singing. Excuse me. It may seem strange for me to weep, even now, even after all this. But it was a happy time. The last happy time.

My brother was jealous of that happiness, for he had found little enough in his own life, despite his wealth, which was far greater than mine, and despite his favored position as firstborn. Perhaps that is why he could not simply be glad for me. Instead, he worked to poison my mind against Melusine.

Yet I must not blame him for my fault. Love should have been enough to shield my heart from his poisonous tongue. But his constant whispers, his sneers, his insinuating questions — they wore away at me as water wears on a rock.

I should never have let him in our home on a Friday night. It was almost defiant of me, I think — a way of showing that I had nothing to hide. But my heart was tender and raw, harrowed by the doubts he had already planted there. So when Melusine excused herself just before midnight, all it took was his raised eyebrow, his amused and scornful grin — not even a grin, just a twitch at the corner of his mouth — to drive me to rash action. In that moment I decided to spy on Melusine, both to quiet my brother, and to set my heart at rest.

I have not known a moment of peace since.

Near the end of my third day in the forest a light rain — little more than a mist, really — began to fall. I stopped to lean against a tree to rest and suddenly I heard the singing, clear and rippling as water over stone.

I knew at once it must be her.

Following the song, as my grandfather had so long ago, I pushed my way through the ferns and bracken. A sudden wall of fog loomed ahead of me. I hesitated, then plunged through — and in that moment knew that I had come to the place I sought.

The land dipped, and I found the closest thing I had yet seen to a trail, a little twisting path that led downward between two ever-steepening banks, mostly rocky but dotted with clusters of fern, of primrose, of eglantine. In the gray light drops of water stood like jewels on their petals.

Beneath her singing, enhancing its beauty like a skilled accompanist, was the crystalline music of flowing, falling water.

The rain stopped. The sun, behind me, was low in the sky. Its rays came sideways through the forest in shafts that limned the ancient trees and seemed to light the soft mist from within, bars of light and darkness alternating.

As I walked the path grew steeper, the banks higher. The light was nearly gone when I stumbled, righted myself, and saw her. Though I had known what to expect, it was all I could do to keep from drawing back, from crying out in astonishment.

Extract from the Testimony of Raymond de Lusignan, as offered to the Abbot of the Monastery of Saint Denis, in the year of Our Lord 953:

Every Friday without fail Melusine retreated, at midnight, to the tower room she had claimed as her own. On that fateful Friday, goaded by my brother, I waited some ten or fifteen minutes after she had climbed the stairs, then mounted to the room myself, my way lit by the torches that burned in the wall mounts.

Her door was closed. I leaned against it. Faintly, I could hear two things — the plash of water, and her singing. A sudden flare of jealousy scalded my heart. Was she singing for someone else?

With the point of my dagger, I widened a hole between two of the planks that made her door. It took time, for I had to work silently. I had not forgotten the promise I made when we married, that I would not ask what she did on Saturdays, or seek to know it in any way — had not forgotten that she had told me that if I broke this vow all our happiness would come to an end. But it seemed, now, in my jealous passion, as if my happiness had ended anyway. And I thought that if I could do this thing in silence, do it without her knowing, and if she proved innocent — as yet more than half of me believed she would — that she would never know, and all might still be well.

At last I finished my work. Returning my dagger to its sheath, I pressed my eye to the hole I had made.

It was all I could do to keep from crying out in horror. I staggered back, then fled down the stairs as silently as I could.

I did not speak of what I had seen. And when Melusine reappeared in her usual form on Sunday she did not act as if she realized that I had spied on her. But despite the fact that I now knew she had not betrayed me with any other lover, it was from that moment that our happiness was doomed.

On the far side of the pool, at the water's edge, sat my grandmother, Melusine.

I had known what to expect, of course. I had read it in the legends, in my grandfather's testimony.

It was something else entirely to see it.

From the waist up, she was, even now, all these centuries later, the most beautiful of women, with abundant tresses of thick, red-gold hair that tumbled past her shoulders, and hid her bare breasts. But from the waist down her body was that of an enormous snake, covered with scales of bluish-gray. It was hard to guess the length of this abomination, for it was coiled beneath her, but I imagine it was fifteen feet at the least.

From her shoulders sprouted a pair of batlike wings, at rest now and folded behind her, yet still terrifying for their demonic-looking points.

She ceased her singing and looked in my direction. Panic seized me. What to do, what to say? After all these years, and even knowing what I would find, I felt as if my tongue had turned to stone.

A look of puzzlement crossed her face. "You can see me!" she said.

"Should I not be able to?" I asked, able to speak at last. I took a step closer.

"It has been a long time since anyone has been able to see me," she answered, stirring the water with the tip of her tail. She sounded nervous, uncertain.

"We share the same blood," I said, by way of explanation.

She slid into the pool — that same pool where my grandfather had first met her, first fallen in love with her — and swam in my direction, her head well above the water, the great tail pushing her forward.

I thought of what I carried in my pack, and felt a moment of uncertainty myself. Even in this form my grandmother was the most enchanting woman I had ever seen. Now that I had seen her, could I really give her what I had spent so long in search of?

What does he want, this strange young man? And why does he look so familiar? She knows that face, those eyes, from so long ago.

He does not fear her. He even seems pleased to see her. And yet, somehow, he fills her with dread.

No, not merely dread. Anticipation. What strange thing does he — wait! Now she knows who he looks like.

It's Geoffroi! Her poor, strange, horrid Geoffroi. Not him, of course. And that terrible tusk is gone. But even so, he's near enough to be . . . his son?

Now memory floods Melusine, and she remembers all unwillingly what happened after that fateful night when Raymond spied on her in her bath. She had known he had done it, of course — had felt a cold chill in her spine the moment his eye fell on her.

But she had not spoken of it, hoping that if his betrayal remained secret that the doom she carried would not be stirred.

the hardest, kindest gift

Here is how my faithlessness was revealed:

In the weeks that followed my spying on Melusine I tried to pretend that it had not happened. Yet the closeness we had once enjoyed now seemed forced and stiff.

I have thought about this much in the years since I came here to the monastery, where there is so much time to think, and I begin to wonder if in every marriage there are things that should remain secret. How much of ourselves can we really share? Is anyone ever ready to see the all of it, the deep and secret parts that we ourselves sometimes fear to peek at?

I do not know the answer. But I do know this: Whether or not there are things that should not be known, there are things that should not be said, words that once they poison the air can never be taken back, but hang like a curtain of venom between you and the one you love.

Thus it was with me and Melusine when we learned of Geoffroi's crime against the monastery.

From the moment that I discovered Melusine's secret I had begun to think about the boys, of course. It seemed clear that their strangeness had come from . . . from whatever she was. I loved them none the less. But now I worried about them. And the whispers that I had shut out for the last many years began to pierce my defenses, to land like arrows on my heart. "They are demon seed," the wagging tongues said. "The proud blood of Lusignan is tainted now and forevermore."

Which is why, I confess, when word came of Geoffroi's atrocity, my first, horrified reaction was not sorrow for the lives lost, but shame for my own family. In a moment of black rage I turned on Melusine and cried, "Foul serpent, you have contaminated the blood of a noble line!"

Would that someone had cut my living tongue from my mouth before I uttered those loveless words.

Melusine shrieked and bolted from the room. At first I thought that terrible cry, torn from her heart and echoing still in my ears today, was one of rage. All too soon I realized it came from terror and sorrow.

She ran for her tower room. I sprang up to pursue her, but she was faster than I, as she always had been.

She did not go all the way to her room. Halfway up the long, winding stair she sprang to the sill of a window — her foot impressed itself into the solid stone, leaving a deep print — and flung herself out.

I was but an arm's length behind her. Horrified, I leaned over the sill, expecting to find her dashed to her death on the rocks below.

What I saw was even worse. Suspended in midair, my beloved wife was writhing and twisting and crying out in pain.

Her clothes vanished in a burst of blue flame and then, before my very eyes, her human shape was stripped away as her legs fused into a single thick trunk that lengthened and lengthened, stretching beneath her in loathsome coils. Blue-gray scales slid across its surface, as if she were being sheathed in armor by some invisible smith. She cried out as leathery wings ripped their way from her shoulders. Then she began to cough, a horrible, wracking spasm. Finally some small black thing burst forth from her mouth and fluttered away. In that moment she stretched her arms toward me longingly, as if she wanted me to take her back somehow. I had my foot on the sill, and was ready to leap out into her embrace, heedless of my own life, when she was caught as if by an invisible hand and yanked away from me.

That was the last I ever saw of her, though I heard her again, wailing her warning around the castle towers whenever death was near.

He has my mother's eyes, *thinks Melusine, as she stares at the young man who has invaded her grotto.*

Those eyes frighten her, stirring, as they do, so many memories.

When did it begin, *she asks herself,* this long, long curse? What were its roots?

She knows it was not in the moment of Raymond's betrayal, horrible as that was.

Perhaps it was when she had refused to choose sides in that most ancient of wars, the battle that sundered heaven when Lucifer took arms against his creator and shook the foundations of the world. The rebel angels were hurled out. The faithful angels were kept in. But those who would not take a side, who understood the root of Lucifer's discontent but could not rise against the one who had made them, they had their own doom, and were flung to Earth, where they became the deathless folk of faerie, the dangerously beautiful ones who lived their own life at the edge of reality as humans knew it, yet could not end their fascination with mortals, so fragile and yet so blessed in their ability to die.

She was one of those fallen ones, and for her crime she carried this curse: That one day of the week she would be half serpent, and that this doom would be eternal, unless she could find a man who would promise never to seek to learn her secret. If they married, and he was faithful for all their time together, then she would be granted mortality, and a peaceful rest at last. But if that man failed, then all happiness would end, and she must take her serpent form forever, and ever, and ever.

Unless . . .

My grandmother. My grandmother. Her hooded eyes gaze up at me, the strange vertical pupils only making her more beautiful. But then her forked tongue flicks out from between her shapely lips, and my fascination turns to horror. Why that one thing, above all others, should disgust me I am not certain. Perhaps it is because in other ways her human and serpent parts are clearly distinct. But that flickering tongue darting from those human lips makes shudderingly real the curse that lies upon her.

We talked for hours as the moon rose above the still waters of her pool. Much of that talk was of my father, the last of her children to die, and his many attempts to redeem himself in the centuries that followed his burning of the monastery.

She had attended his death, of course, as she had those of all her children.

She had always known when death, denied to her, was coming for one she loved.

Though three hundred years had passed, I still shuddered at the memory of her shrieks and wails as she circled in the night air outside our walls, warning that my father's last hour was drawing near.

Finally she asked the question I was waiting for. Putting a hand on my knee, she said, "Why have you sought me out, Geoffroi? Why now, after all these years?"

"I have a gift for you."

She looked at me in surprise.

I reached into my pack and withdrew the glass cube. I unwrapped it slowly, wondering, even now, if I were doing the right thing. But she had seen it, and the hungry look in her eyes reassured me.

She extended her hands for it, and her tongue — which she had tried to keep under control after she realized how it bothered me — flicked eagerly in and out of her mouth.

"Do you know what this is?" she asked, scarcely able to contain her joy.

"I know that in the moment of your final transformation you lost more than just your human shape."

"Much more," she said sorrowfully, her tail coiling just beneath the surface of the moonlit water. "I lost the very gift I had gained by marrying a human — my mortality."

She smiled, a sad, brave look that nearly broke my heart.

"You mortals think it would be so fine to live forever. But there comes a time when it is time to go, when one would gladly welcome death's cold embrace."

In the glass cube the black thing fluttered, the small but missing part of her that I had spent so many years tracking down.

Its tiny face was the image of hers.

Without another word she lifted the box and smashed it against a rock.

The little winged thing flew up and attached itself to her face. Her eyes widened in fear, but only for a moment. Gasping, she breathed in — and in it went. A cry escaped her, a mingled sound of pain and relief. Her tail began to thrash violently, beating the water into a foam.

And then, in only a moment, the centuries caught up with her.

Like my grandfather before me, I watched Melusine's transformation in fascinated horror — though this was a far different transformation. Her skin began to wither and wrinkle. Her golden hair turned the color of ashes. Her wings crumbled like dry leather, dropping in brittle flakes to the water's surface.

Slowly the great serpentine tail ceased its writhing.

It didn't take much longer. Soon there was nothing left of her but a scattering of dust — dust, and a blue diaphanous sheath, like that which is left behind when a snake sheds its skin.

I still have that sheath, which I carefully rolled up and tucked into my pack.

When I finished that task, I looked up and saw through tear-dimmed eyes that her pool had disappeared. All that was left of our encounter, scattered among the dried leaves at my feet, were sparkling shards of broken glass — the fragile wrapping that had held the hardest, kindest gift I ever gave.

about the authors

BRUCE COVILLE has published over eighty books for young readers, including *Goblins in the Castle* and *My Teacher Is an Alien*. His recent writing for Scholastic includes *Into the Land of the Unicorns* and *Song of the Wanderer*, the first two books of his ongoing series, THE UNICORN CHRONICLES. Bruce lives in Syracuse, New York, with his wife and sometime illustrator, Katherine Coville; a varying number of children and semi-demented cats; and Thor, the jet-propelled Norwegian elkhound.

GREGORY MAGUIRE is the author of a dozen books for young readers, including THE HAMLET CHRONICLES, the most recent installment of which is *Four Stupid Cupids*. His books for adults include *Confessions of an Ugly Stepsister* and *Wicked: The Life and Times of the Wicked Witch of the West*, a novel about Oz. When he had finished writing *Wicked*, Gregory entertained the notion of a sequel. "Scarecrow" has metamorphosed from scenes from that unpublished novel. The rest of the book, he claims, "has been sensibly retired to a very deep dark place in the back of a file drawer in an underground bunker in a town too far away for you to have heard of it." His fans hope that he will reconsider.

D. J. MALCOLM has been writing stories since she was six years old. She has spent most of her bipedal days in school or working in bookstores, confirming her belief that the three best things in the world are books, books, and books. Now she is busy raising a husband and three children, but she has a really cool office in her basement, behind the furnace, next to the water heater, over the sump pump. She hates cold weather and mosquitoes, and is currently a suffering artist in Minneapolis, Minnesota.

Illinois resident JUDE MANDELL has been writing fiction and nonfiction for young readers for several years. An adjunct faculty member of Eastern Illinois University, Jude has also worked with Chicago's famed The Second City theatre, writing and performing for their children's productions. She has appeared in summer stock, opera, and musical theater. (Her favorite role was Luisa in *The Fantasticks,* which she played for over two years in Philadelphia.)

TAMORA PIERCE is the wildly popular author of nearly twenty fantasy novels for young readers, including the SONG OF THE LIONESS quartet, the CIRCLE OF MAGIC series, and another series called THE IMMORTALS. Her books have appeared in English, Swedish, German, and Danish. She lives in New York City with her beloved Spouse-Creature Tim Leibe in a shoebox apartment, which they share with three cats, two parakeets, and wildlife rescued from the park. "Elder

Brother," her story for this collection, is about a tree mentioned at the end of her novel *Wolf-Speaker*.

LAWRENCE SCHIMEL grew up surrounded by animals, both domestic (horses, goats, chickens, ferrets, and llamas, to name a few) and wild (foxes, pheasants, flying squirrels, etc.). He enjoys learning languages and traveling, and has at various times studied flamenco dancing, played polo, and made blown-glass art. A full time author and anthologist, his short stories and poems have appeared in numerous magazines and over 150 anthologies. His books for adults include *Camelot Fantastic*, *Tarot Fantastic*, and *Fields of Blood: Vampire Stories from the Heartland*. Lawrence currently divides his time between New York City and Madrid, Spain.

JANNI LEE SIMNER grew up in New York, and might have stayed there if not for a trip to Wyoming the year she turned fourteen. She's been on the move ever since — living in Missouri before settling in Arizona, and camping throughout the United States. She has published three novels: *Ghost Horse*, *The Haunted Trail*, and *Ghost Vision*, as well as more than two dozen short stories, which have appeared in such places as *Girl's Life Magazine*, *A Glory of Unicorns*, and *Bruce Coville's Book of Magic*.

Self-confessed pizza junkie NANCY SPRINGER lives in Pennsylvania where she has produced award-winning books for adults, children, and young adults. Her numerous accolades include an Edgar Award in 1995 from the Mystery Writers of America for her young adult novel *Toughing It* and a Nebula from the Science Fiction Writers of America for her short story, "The Boy Who Plaited Manes." Nancy's recent books include *I Am Morgan LeFay*, a companion novel to the critically acclaimed *I Am Mordred*.

TIM WAGGONER lives in Ohio with two daughters (ages six and one as of this writing), two cats (ages uncertain), and one wife (age classified). He teaches creative writing at Sinclair Community College. He has published two novels, a short-story collection, and over sixty short stories. His previous works for young readers can be found in *Bruce Coville's UFOs* and *Bruce Coville's Book of Nightmares 2*.

JANE YOLEN says, "Writers are themselves half-human. One half is Muse, the other Flat-footed Folk. I live in my head part-time and the rest of the time either in Massachusetts or Scotland. But because I have three granddaughters, I also spend time in Myrtle Beach, South Carolina, and Minneapolis, Minnesota. In between I write, write, write. I have written more than 200 books, so I must be musing a lot. You can find out about my books at www.janeyolen.com." Jane has won a list of awards that would fill this page, and her recent picture book, *How Do Dinosaurs Say Goodnight?*, was a *New York Times* bestseller.